DEDICATION

To my nieces and nephews...
May I be that inspiration to you that lets you all know that you can achieve anything in this world. May you fulfill all of your dreams, and reach all of your goals...

To my grandfather Alberto Antolin Sabio, my uncle Raul "Tio Rigo" Mejia, and my dear mother Raquel Felipa Sabio...
May I make you smile down on me from the ancestral realm. I hope that I am making all of you very proud with my literary accomplishments...

To Tatayana "Yana" Gee...
Thank you for all of the love and support that you've given me. Thank you for the friendship that we have, and allowing me to be a part of your life. Thank you for all of the vulnerable moments that we've shared, and allowing me to bond with you. I feel honored to be able to witness the beautiful queen that you've grown to become. I treasure your presence in my life, and hope that I make you proud. Te amo mucho, Cuteness...

The Chronicles of The Black Fist: F.U.R.I. of The People
[Book II]
© Copyright 2019
Written by Kevin Alberto Sabio

CHAPTER 1

Night has fallen over New Washington City, illuminating the evening skyline with bright florescent lights. Metro New Washington is especially lit up, serving as a beacon of progress and upward mobility, the crown jewel of the city's vibrancy. The power elites of the city move about, either exiting their halls of financial power to call it a night, or staying in to close out power deals to bring added financial prosperity to themselves and their company. Luxury cars and limousines zip through the streets of Metro New Washington, transporting their passengers to and fro, casting snakes of red tail lights or white headlights about, adding to the illumination of the city's night sky. They snake their way through the city, heading to the surrounding suburbs located either in the north or the south of the city, creating a bit of a lull in the city. A few of the surrounding buildings are blackened out, their inhabitants having left for the night, save only for the presence of overnight security guards, and cleaning crews.

The Comfort Cove Inn sits sleepily on the corner of Washington Boulevard and Capital Street in Metro New Washington, surrounded by a few grandiose luxury high rise complexes; one of the newer ones that was erected in recent years as a part of the 'renaissance' of New Washington City. It's become a magnet in attracting business people to the city, as well as for more 'upscale' nefarious types that use the hotel for ulterior purposes. It's long been rumored that high end escorting takes place there, used to woo both business and political elites for the benefit of the city, if not mainly themselves. But of course, with the local law enforcement, they would never do anything to disrupt the powers that control the city, biting the proverbial hand that feeds them. Don't ask, don't tell as they say...

On one of the upper floors, a group of about twelve men are having a clandestine meeting in one of their conference rooms. Six heavily armed beefy white men are stationed inside, all wearing earpieces and carrying handguns, stoically standing guard. There are four others stationed outside of the room, all wearing shades and looking quite nefarious, their own handguns clipped to their holsters on their sides. The angry pale faces of the men inside contort with rage, as they converse among themselves. "It's been well over twenty years...", Adolphus spits out in his heavily Afrikaans-accented English, "...And the Blacks have ruined our country! It's about time we took matters into our own hands, and took our country *back*!". The other men in the room murmur in agreement, nodding their approval. They had secretly left their home country of South Africa to hold this meeting, and plan out their strategy to gain 'their' country back. Though the Afrikaners still controlled most of the business and industry in the country, and probably all of the land, they still felt that their way of life had been irrevocably compromised with the transition of power to the native South Africans. They wanted things to go back to the way they were before the power transfer, and were apparently more than ready to fight for it. Francois nods in agreement. "That is right", he concedes, "Things have gotten worse since they took over. We've had nothing but strikes, unrest, and recessions since they took over. This needs to change...*now!*".

"...Yes!"

"...Here, here!"

"...Of course!"

"...No more!"

"No longer should we suffer under the porous rule of these wretched Blacks! We need to take our country back, and we need to do that *now*! The sooner, the better!"

The men murmur in agreement again, with some of them clapping their support. All of a sudden, they then hear movement coming from above them. They look up, at first surprised, and then concerned. The security men with their shades look up at the ceiling, slowly reaching for their weapons.

"What was *that*...?"

"...I don't know. It's coming from above us..."

"Could they have found out about this meeting?"

"...Impossible! But, you know how these Black are..."

"...Yes, they can have spies everywhere, especially these American Blacks. They can be *beyond* arrogant..."

Adolphus turns to one of the Security Men. "Do they see anyone out front...?", he asks.

"No one is out there...", he replies, after a moment on his earpiece, "The hallway is clear...not so much as a cleaning lady..."

"This floor is supposed to be closed off..."

"...We were assured anonymity."

"Let's all just relax...", Francois says, "It's probably nothing-..."

All of a sudden, a person drops in on them from the ceiling out of nowhere, landing in a crouched position on the circular table that they're all seated at. They are all shocked to see this individual, apparently female, dressed in white and black of Egyptian design, with golden arm bands and choker. Her black cat-head shaped helmet mask intently stares at them, burning into their souls, filling them with feelings of dread and impending doom. Before they even have any time to react, the unknown assailant jerks her head towards the armed guards, and flings throwing knives at each of the six security men in the room, immediately incapacitating them.

Whiiiiiiiiiiisssssszzz!!

Thok...thok...thok...thok...thok...thok!

They don't even have time to reach for their guns, instantly falling before the others.

The twelve seated men look on aghast, first at their fallen security, and then at this unknown assailant, now full of dread. "Who-...?!", Adolphus barely gets out.

"<....-You will all *die!*>"

They all cringe, not knowing what was just said to them in that eerie, synthesized voice, not recognizing the language being spoken to them by this killer. Sekhmet Baset just stares them down, her shimmering emerald eyes now focused on slaughtering every last man in this room. She jerks her head immediately towards her right, and goes after those men seated right there, throwing kicks at their heads, and throwing herself into battle. She moves so quickly and effortlessly, instantly taking them down, battering them about, and breaking bones. She then jerks her head towards the head of the table, and sees Adolphus seated by the head of the table. He immediately turns to make a run for the door, trying to escape the carnage that she's inflicting. She leaps towards him, jumping over the table, and catches him before he reaches the door.

"Help-...!", Adolphus tries to cry out.

Sekhmet Baset grabs him from behind, takes his head in her hands, and viciously snaps his neck, causing him to lifelessly fall forward.

KRAK!!!

His body hits the doors of the room with a hard thud. She then twists her body out of the way, avoiding the opening doors of the conference room. The four guards stationed outside bust their way inside, aiming their guns into the room. They are shocked to see the bodies of their dead comrades lying lifelessly on the floor, and that of the body of Adolphus at their feet. Sekhmet Baset unsheaths her short Khopesh sword from her back, and slices off the arms of the nearest guard. He lets out a short-lived scream, as she instantly finishes him off by lobbing his head off.

"Aaaaah-...!"

...-CHOK!!!

As if the world existed in slow motion, the other three guards turn towards their fallen comrade, as his body falls toward the floor, and Sekhmet Baset moves in on them to finish the carnage...

*   *   *   *   *   **

Detective Amirah Umi arrives at the Comfort Cove Inn, making her way through the patrolmen and hotel security already on the scene in the lobby. She flashes her badge to a few uniforms on hand, and they permit her to pass. She finally makes her

way upstairs to the floor of the crime scene, and is surprised to see so many people

there, as she exits the elevator. Her eyebrows furrow when she sees a few members of

the brass on hand, murmuring among themselves, wearing concerned looks on their

faces. *Uh oh...*, she thinks to herself, *you KNOW it's not a good sign when the brass is*

on hand before the investigation even starts.... She makes her way into the conference

room, and is shocked to see the carnage. There are bodies all over the room, with blood

spatter going everywhere. It takes her a second to regain her composure, and sees a

familiar forensics specialist. They share a familiar smile.

"...Detective Umi!"

"...What have you got?"

"Twenty-two bodies...blunt force trauma...some were dismembered..."

"Any suspects...?"

"...None. Whoever did this is in the wind..."

Amirah goes over to the nearest victim, and inspects him. He was beaten up pretty bad,

according to the bruises on his body, and you could tell that some of his bones were

broken. She lets out a heavy sigh. "Any ID on the victims...?", she asks.

"Apparently...they were all South African nationals."

"...Really?!", she replies, surprised, looking at her.

"...Yep. And...they weren't registered as guests here at the hotel, either..."

"...*That* doesn't make much sense!" She briefly pauses. "...Not unless they were planning something illegal, or seditious..."

"...You really think so?"

Amirah gives her a sarcastic look, raising her eyebrow. "A bunch of Afrikaners having a *secret* meeting at a hotel that they're not even staying at...? *Please* don't tell me that you're actually *that* gullible...".

The forensics tech just shrugs her shoulders. Amirah just shakes her head, rising. She beings to exit the room. "Get me the usual...DNA...prints...the works. The *last* thing I need is some samurai Whodini messing up my streets". "You got it, Detective", she answers. Amirah started to get a really bad feeling, as she starts to leave the hotel. It was bad enough that her job had been wearing on her more and more these last few years; the changes within the department, and on the political landscape had taken a bit of a toll on her. It seems as if that reprieve that she'd had about giving up her badge was coming to an end, since it seemed to tug at her more and more every day. Other than her clandestine relationship/partnership with The Black Fist, she questioned her desire to remain on the force more and more every day. Had it not been for their meeting up, she probably would've resigned a long time ago. Amirah lets out another heavy sigh as she enters the elevator. She pushes the button, and the doors slowly close on her. *Lets hope that this case won't be as bad as I think it will be...*, she thinks to herself.

CHAPTER 2

Nyerere is in Southern Douglas Heights, wrapping up his latest history class at Woodson-Rogers College, much to his students' dismay. They loved his class, and felt that he was a great addition to the campus. He was still young enough that his students could relate to him, but was very well versed in his subject matter, and made his classes very interesting. He had to give credit to Dr. Oduno for continuing to recruit him to join their campus, even when he didn't have any desire to do so whatsoever, beforehand. This opportunity had opened up so many doors for him, especially with the publishing of his book "*The Chronicles of The Black Fist*"; the ability to have the school help him to promote it, the people that he's been able to meet and network with, traveling across the country and abroad. He had to admit, he felt blessed to be reaching his thirty-first birthday today, and to have achieved all that he has, up to this point. He's been able to do much these past four years here on campus; helping to build stronger ties between the school, the community, and Africana P.R.I.D.E., even helping to revive some of the old programs and initiatives that the organization has. He was proudest to have helped revive parts of the UNEEC network, even helping to establish the college's Anderson-Clingman School of Business and Economics based in Turner Heights, helping to revitalize, not only that community, but also some of the growing small businesses in the city. He truly wished that his parents had been able to live to see him reach these accomplishments, though he knew that they were watching him, and smiling from the ancestral realm.

Nyerere finally finishes up his lesson, and his students are now exiting the classroom. He was happy to have had a good class, and wanted to finish the day on a positive note; Mama Tabula and Baba Balogun were going to meet up with him for a late birthday lunch, and then they were going to swing back to the campus to hear a spiritual comrade of Tehuti's and Waset speak; Imakhu Senefra Atenhotep was a revered leader in the Kemetic spiritual community, and was a highly sought after activist speaker, and priestess. It was an honor to have her come to New Washington City, and grace them with her wisdom, essence, and guidance. Nyerere looks up, and sees Amirah enter into his classroom. He was surprised to see her, as they don't generally get to see each other much out in public. Amirah sees him, and flashes him a tired smile. "Hey you...", she greets him, "...Happy birthday, Nyerere".

"...Detective Umi! How are you? Thank you so much."

She gives him a hug and peck on the cheek, trying not to linger too long, practicing some self restraint. She continues to wear her tired smile. "Thought that I'd stop by...felt it would be better than a phone call...".

"...I'm glad! It's good anytime I get to see you."

"...Likewise."

"How are things on the force?"

"Oh...you know...", she replies, rolling her eyes.

"...Ouuuch! I was hoping that things would've improved..."

"Yeah, well..."

"...Anything that I can do to help?"

Amirah pauses, looking up at him, and tries to fight off a sly smile trying to form on her face. Things had gotten...*interesting*...between the two of them, over these last few years; going from antagonism, to comrades, to kindred spirits...their lives had become interestingly intertwined, especially after she'd figured out his true identity as The Black Fist. She then clears her throat, becoming a bit more serious, remembering why she came in the first place. "Um...I need to talk to you...".

"Oooooh...can we talk a little later? I'm supposed to be meeting up with Mama Tabula and Baba Balogun for a birthday lunch-..."

"...-The *other* you."

Nyerere pauses, a bit stunned. They *never* discussed his alter ego out in public; that was why they had the secret cellphones. If she came to him in public, it *had* to be serious.

"Not here...", he replies to her, slipping into his infamous gravelly voice. It always threw Amirah whenever he instantly switched personalities like that.

"Where, then?"

"...The parking lot."

"Your car, or mine?"

"...Better make it yours. You can drop me off at the restaurant to meet the elders, and we can talk on the way."

"Okay...that works."

"Great...", He jovially replies, switching back to his normal self, "I'll grab my stuff. The elders would *love* to see you, and say hi..."

Nyerere smiles, and gathers his belongings. Amirah returns a smile of her own. She knew that he would be interested in this case. He was just as much a guardian of the city as she was, if not moreso. They'd been through a lot together; the changing of the political landscape with the election of A. Simi Leishon-Integration as mayor, with Overton "Ovie" Seere being made his new Police Commissioner, and with Joseph "Brutality" Brutus resigning, and going to work for Iggy Norance. And though the new mayor and police commissioner had 'publicly' shut down the Anti-Black Fist Task Force, they were still launching clandestine operations against him. It made their work together a bit more difficult, and called for them to become even more vigilant and adaptable in the ways that they operated. It also called for the need for them to create an alternative information gathering network, an *underground* if you will, in order for them to properly protect the city, and to keep eyes and ears on, not to mention combat, their enemies. It called for a lot of long nights together; planning, researching, and recruiting others to help. They were becoming more than just kindred spirits, at least for her. There were times when she still didn't know where she stood with him; were they just comrades in the struggle, or could there be something more...? Nyerere wasn't like any of the other cops, or DA's that she'd known and dealt with; hell...he wasn't like any of the other *men* that she's ever dealt with, or dated. His history made him intriguing, his intelligence attracting, and his dedication alluring. She couldn't help but get sucked in.

"...Let's go", she says. Knowing what she did about his parents, and what they did for the organization, not to mention the impact that they'd had on so many others, it was no wonder that she was feeling the way she was about him. *He IS his father's son*, she thinks to himself, *no wonder everybody loves him*. She was fighting to keep it professional, but wasn't being very successful. It also didn't help that she'd been in a relationship dry spell for the last few years. She just heavily sighs, as they exit his classroom...

CHAPTER 3

Ignatius "Iggy" Norance V stares out of the window of his high rise office in Metro New Washington. He looks out over the city, his face now grim and stern. His hands are folded behind his back, his mood soured. He is joined in his office by his old friend and business partner, Raymundo "Ray" Sysm, seated in front of his desk. Ray had spent the last few years working closely with Governor Wyatt Supremacy as a lobbyist, and wanted to get back into the private sector, liking the straight-forwardness of the business world, as opposed to the clandestine back alley wheeling and dealing of the politicians. They'd always had a great working relationship with one another, in the past and presently, and Iggy gladly joined forces with Ray again, as well as their two families' long history together. They are also joined by Brutality, who was seated next to Ray. The two men looked quite grim, not really wanting to upset Iggy any more than he already was. "How bad is it...?", Iggy asks.

"...Pretty bad, Mr. Norance...", Brutality replies, "...There were no survivors."

"...How?!"

"No idea. The Commissioner is looking into it-..."

"...-No disrespect to the Commissioner...", Ray snorts, "...But, those people couldn't find a wet napkin in a rain storm!"

"Ovie is good people...", Brutality answers, "...He *won't* let this slide."

"...-Well intentions, and dedication mean *nothing* without results", Iggy snorts, "That's why *you* have *his* old job, and *he* has *yours*. I needed somebody that I know can do the job, and do it *right*."

"We're *both* looking into this. This *won't* go unanswered."

"...We assured them the utmost safety and discretion", Ray says, "This makes us look bad, to have our defenses penetrated like that..."

"I don't like looking weak, gentlemen...", Iggy states, "Find out who did this, and put a stop to them. Whatever leaks exit, plug them up. Tie up any loose ends, and get rid of any weak links."

"...Consider it done", Brutality replies.

Iggy looks over his shoulder, and nods at him. Brutality returns his nod, gets up from his seat, and exits the office. Ray watches him leave, and then turns back to Iggy. "He's loyal, Ig...and looks up to you", he states. "...He's actually *effective*, that's why I brought him in", Iggy replies, "I couldn't have what happened last time, happening again", he says, referencing The Black Fist.

"He's *still* giving you trouble, Ig...?", Ray asks, raising an eyebrow.

"...From time to time. It's quite infuriating..."

"...Damn savages! Give them an inch, and they become a pugnacious lot!"

"What happened to those Afrikaners is bad for business. They were always supportive of us in the past..."

"...I know! Do you think that he's behind it?"

"...I wouldn't put it past him. He's usually only this brutal when it comes to his own people..."

"Yes, those savages *are* a vicious lot..."

"...-I want him crushed! There's no love lost between him, and Brutality. This should be interesting..."

"...Seems like I chose the right time to leave the political arena, my friend."

"Speaking of which...have you talked to our illustrious mayor, recently?"

"...A. Simi? Why, yes, I have."

"So...what do you think of our boy?"

"...Definitely *not* what I expected. For a savage, he's rather...tamed."

"...That's why we put him into office. He lets us do our thing, and keeps the savages at bay. Even the wilder ones don't cross him."

Both men snicker at his comment. The activist community hadn't had very much success when challenging A. Simi on certain matters of public policy. Some of the city's residents had gotten down right hostile with them, until it was too late. Many big businesses have moved in, and a number of neighborhoods have become gentrified under A. Simi's administration, pushing out a lot of long-time residents and businesses.

The rising rents, and incoming transplants and gentrifiers from the outlying counties were now changing the face of some of the historically Black neighborhoods of New Washington City. This new age of prosperity had come with a price for the local residents; obviously a price that they couldn't afford. Only *now* were they starting to look to support the local activists in their fight to preserve their communities, and stave off gentrification. Of course, the damage had already be done, and some of this fightback was coming too little, too late. It made Iggy smile at the gullibility of the locals, and their political ignorance. They had nobody to blame but themselves. They were *such* an ignorant, childish lot...

Ray rises from his seat, which causes Iggy to turn around. "Business to attend to...?", he asks. "Actually, yes...", Ray says, "Trying to close on this property in Turner Heights. Because the savages have ruined the neighborhood so badly...they're selling it for dirt cheap. I'm thinking of converting it into luxury condos...".

"Good luck! That's prime real estate!"
"Yes...we can *finally* get rid of the riff raff from there, and finally have some *quality* residents living there..."
"...At a prime location, too. It's near the subway."
"...Even better. Let me know how it goes."

Ray nods to him, and exits the office. Iggy turns back to his window, a smile now forming on his face. How the savages have squandered the resources of the city, and left the likes of him and his fraternal order to pick up the pieces, and clean everything up, afterward. *Life on top is good...*, he thinks to himself.

CHAPTER 4

Nyerere was trying to put up a jovial front, but was having a hard time maintaining it. He was at the Sankofa-Ifa Community Center, enjoying a bit of an afterparty with Imakhu Senefra Atenhotep. They were there to jointly celebrate his birthday, and Imakhu Senefra's visit to the city. It was hard for him to enjoy the festivities, with what Amirah had told him. He wasn't fazed by the murder of those Afrikaners; quite the opposite. They'd gotten what they deserved; if not for what they were there planning for, then probably for what they had done in the past during their reign in power. He just didn't like the fact that someone was coming into his city, and killing people. He was so caught up in his own thoughts, that he didn't even sense Ife coming up to him.

"Hey, brother! Are you alright...?"

"...Ife! How are you sister?"

"Doing good, brother. Happy birthday, Nyerere!"

She gives him a kiss on the cheek, and an affectionate hug, holding on for a prolonged period of time. Nyerere lets an embarrassed smile slip out, knowing what that long hug was about. With Ife taking over as Director of the Uhuru Shule Academy, the burdens that Nyerere had once faced, now fell onto her. He would still help her out as much as he could, coming by to assist whenever he was available. One night he had stayed late, helping her after a Veneral Equinox concert that they'd held with the children. He was helping her to put some stuff away in her office, which was *his* old office, and the space was quite tight. The constant rubbing and bumping up against each other proved to be too much for either of them, and they both finally caved into their secret carnal desire for each other. It was truly a wonderful, intimate experience to have shared with each other, but they chose never to pursue it much further, afterward.

"...Thank you so much, sister!"

"*Pleeease* tell me that you're doing okay? You had that same look on your face like when we used to work together..."

"I'm fine, sister...I promise."

"Okay..."

She finally releases him, flashing him a reassuring smile. He returns his own reassuring smile, holding her hands in his. He was truly glad to see her again, and glad that she came out for his birthday. "I assure you, sister...you have *nothing* to worry about. I am happy, and stress free". Ife nods in return. "That's good to know, brother", she returns, "I don't want to have to cut nobody...". Nyerere returns a laugh, causing Ife to beam even more. They truly missed seeing each other every day, and working together. Of course, recruiting trips to the school always gave him an excuse to come by the campus, and spend time with Ife and the students.

"Have you had the chance to meet Imakhu Senefra?"

"Actually, no."

"...Would you like to?"

"...Of course! I absolutely *love* her! I have all her books, and CDs!"

"Let's go..."

They walk over to where Senefra is seated, seeing her warm brown face beaming at the crowd present. She had a motherly spirit to her, so regal and proud. She was talking with Waset and Tabula, enjoying some organic fruit juice. As Nyerere approaches her, her brown face smiles at him. "Hetepu, Nyerere! How are you? Earthday blessings, young brother".

"...Imakhu Senefra, thank you so much! I really enjoyed your lecture this evening." She puts her hand to her heart, and bows. "Dua, young brother."

"Imakhu Senefra...I'd like to introduce you to my friend Ife Ochoa."

"Hetepu, Imakhu Senefra,", Ife coos, "It's a pleasure to meet you!"

"Hetepu, dear sister. The honor is mine."

"I'm a huge fan of your work!"

"Dua, sister. It's great to know that our work is having an impact."

The two women continue to converse. Nyerere smiles, glad to be seeing everything going as well as they are. He greatly respected Imakhu Senefra, and had read many of her works. He was glad that he was able to work something out with the college, and be able to bring her to the campus, with the much added help of Tehuti and Waset; it was their friendship with her that made this all possible. She looked so regal in her priestly purple robe, her greying locks accenting her Kemetic attire. Though she did look a bit fatigued, her golden ornaments helped to brighten her appearance, and add youth to her elderly face. Traveling all over the country and world, administering to so many followers...it must take its toll on you physically.

"...-Mut!"

They all turn towards the entrance of the center. They see a striking dark chocolate young sister, around Nyerere's age, approaching their position, sporting the same Kemetic-styled dress as Senefra, beaming with joy and pride. This draws a joyous smile out of Senefra, as she rises from her seat, excitedly extending her arms.

"...Nefertara! You made it!"

"Hetepu, mut...", she joyously greets her in return, "...I just got into town!"

The two women joyously and affectionately embrace each other. Everyone else looks on bewildered, watching the two women smiling and enjoying each others presence. Imakhu Senefra then turns to the others, affectionately taking the young lady's hand.

"...I am so grateful to the neteru! They have brought me back my daughter, Nefertara! It has been a while since we've had the chance to spend some time together! Thanks to Heru for watching over her...she's been able to come and join me here!"

The other party attendees go over to her, greeting her and introducing themselves, bidding her welcome. Nyerere is struck at how attractive she is; her smooth, dark chocolate skin tone accented by her outfit and golden jewelry. Whereas her mother Senefra had long locks, Nefertara sported a short cropped cut. She had a wonderful smile, and emitted great positive energy. He was so taken in by her beauty, that he didn't even notice Nzinga walking up to him.

"...Happy birthday, Nyerere!"

Nyerere turns to her, now surprised. It takes him a second to realize that she is talking to him, and then flashes her a smile. It had been a while since they'd seen each other, with their schedules being so hectic. Their own on again-off again romance made it difficult for them to really spend any quality time together; she, always chasing down some story or his alter ego, or he with his crime fighting, touring, and classes. There was no animosity between them, but their time away from each other did leave the relationship strained. They had felt it best to just remain dear friends. "Hey, sister...", he replies, giving her a hug and kiss on the cheek, "...Thanks! I'm glad that you were able to make it out".

"I wouldn't miss this, despite everything."

"...I hear ya."

"So...", she says, turning to the crowd around Nefertara, "Who's the celebrity?"

"...Oh! Apparently...Imakhu Senefra's daughter came into town to surprise her..."

"...Really? I didn't even know that she *had* any children..."

"...Neither did I. And apparently, not very many other people did, either..."

"Have you met her, yet?"

"...Actually, no."

"...Oh. Cause, from the way that you were staring at her with your mouth all open, I thought that maybe she was an ex that you weren't expecting to see..."

Nyerere returns a sheepish grin to her, now feeling quite embarrassed. Nzinga wears a sly smile, knowing that she'd caught him off guard. *Good thing that she's not the jealous type*, he thinks to himself.

"Damn...busted. You caught that, huh?"

"Hey, what can I say", she laughs, brushing her locks aside, "She *is* quite beautiful. Can't be mad at ya..."

"Thanks."

"Hey...*I* didn't hold up *my* end of this relationship, either. Mama shoulda handled her business to keep daddy at home..."

"Thanks", he says, flashing a reassuring smile, "I'm glad that we can still be friends."

"You're a wonderful brother, Nyerere...the right sister *will* eventually snatch you up."

Nyerere was thankful to Nzinga for being so understanding. Not too many women in her position would've taken the same route, wanting to still remain friends. They cared very deeply for one another, and wished nothing but the best for each other. The timing just happened to be off for them; her journalism career for her, and his crime fighting for him. "So...", she asks, "Should we go, and introduce ourselves?".

"...Let's."

They go to join the small crowd gathered around Senefra and Nefertara. Both women seemed to be very happy to be back around each other. Mother and daughter both continue to hold each others' hands, as they greet the other guests there, reaffirming their bond to each other. It momentarily drew a sense of longing in Nyerere, wishing for his own parents to still be present in his life. Would they be proud of him? How differently would his life had turned out? Would he still have pursued his alternate lifestyle as The Black Fist, if they hadn't died? So many questions and emotions flooded his mind, by the time they got the chance to speak to the two.

"Hetepu, Imakhu..."

"...Hetepu, Nyerere!"

"Imakhu...I'd like to introduce you to another sister that I know. This is Nzinga Zulu...a star journalist at The Griot's Call here in New Washington City..."

"...Hetepu, sister."

"It's an honor to meet you, Imakhu Senefra."

"Nyerere, I'd like to introduce you to my daughter, Nefertara...*also* an academic."

"Hetepu, dear sister."

"Dua, brother...", she replies, intently smiling at him, "...Happy earthday!"

"Thank you, sister."

"Please, brother...call me Nefertara."

"Sure...Nefertara", he replies, smiling.

"I've read your book, brother. *Fascinating* research!"

"Why, thank you, sister!"

"It's similar to a lot of the work that I do myself..."

"Oh, really?"

"Yes...except I focus more on the holistic health side of it...picking up where my mut left off..."

"That's wonderful! I know that the Imakhu must be *immensely* proud of you..."

"I would love to discuss it with you further, some time."

"...I'd like that."

"How were you able to come up with the concept for it, as well as being able to make the connections back to the exact style based on the continent...?"

"Oh....well, *that* actually took a bit more work..."

"...Really? How so...?"

Nyerere and Nefertara continue on with their discussion, now oblivious to the others around them. They continue to discuss academic theory, and their respective fields of research and study, swapping information and war stories. Their intense connection to each other is quite obvious, causing both Senefra and Tabula to watch on with big smiles on their faces. Nzinga just heavily sighs, watching on with a weary smile on her own face, reminiscently shaking her head.

CHAPTER 5

Amirah and The Black Fist are at his headquarters in the Warehouse District, discussing the details of her most recent case; another murder victim was found again, sometime last night. This time, it was a White nationalist group coming into town, looking to do some recruiting, and open up a local chapter. They had been known to be quite violent, especially towards burgeoning immigrant communities. Knowing about the financial transformations taking place in the city, they felt that now would be the perfect time for them to establish a chapter here in the city. Apparently, someone had found out about their plans, and had put an immediate end to them, in the most vicious of fashions. This was causing a lot of angst among the detectives on the force; this killer had struck down questionable elements within their city within a matter of days of each other. They didn't know if this was a serial killer, or some sort of professional assassin trying to start a race war in New Washington City. Either way, it was bad for the city to have this going on, *especially* during this time of economic renaissance. The *last* thing that they needed was some maniac going on a killing spree to scare off the investors, and transplant residents.

As Amirah is debriefing him, The Black Fist seemed somewhat distant and distracted, almost as if he was tuning her out. It bothered her that he was doing that; she had *no choice* but to miss his birthday party last night, and he should have understood that. Her duties as a police officer took her away, when she would have loved nothing more than to be in attendance, and Amirah felt that he shouldn't be holding that against her.

"Fist...are you even *listening*?!"

"...Mmmm..."

""Look, I already *told* you...I couldn't make it. I got called away on a case...*this* case!"

"...Huh?"", he finally says, turning to her, and coming to.

"*Really*, Fist?! You're not even listening to me...!"

"...I'm sorry...just have some stuff on my mind..."

"Yeah...*apparently*", she says, her attitude apparent.

His eyebrows furrowed a bit, caught off guard by her reaction. He didn't understand where this hostility was coming from with her. Things *did* sometimes get complicated between them, ever since she'd found out his identity. There were times when the lines got blurred between their relationship with each other.

"Look...what are you getting so bent out of shape for?! These are *racists* that are getting whacked here...*not* really on the top of my priorities list...!"

"...-Because it's happening here in *our* city! Not to mention...certain people are trying to pin this on *you*!"

"...-I have *nothing* to do with this! Not to mention...this is not even my M.O.!"

"...-*I* know that! *The media* is trying to paint *you* as the killer..."

"...-The *mainstream* media...the one that has *never* supported what I do, nor our people, in the first place!!"

"...-They're not the *only* ones! The mayor and commissioner would *love* to pin this on you, if we can't find the actual killer soon..."

"...-*Please*! They'd blame me for the high cost of *gas* if they could..."

"...-All the more reason to find this wacko, and put him away!"

"Look...do I like the killings...? No. *BUT*...I'm also *not* going to lose any sleep over these racists catching a dirt nap! Afrikaners plotting a government overthrow, and a violent White nationalist group trying to form a chapter here in the city...?! This guy did us all a *favor*..."

"...-*Maybe* if you were focusing more on this case, instead of your little girlfriend, you *might* have a better understanding of the situation!"

This causes The Black Fist to pause, now becoming angry. He didn't like it when she dragged his personal life into these discussions whenever they had operational disagreements. She had crossed that line, and was doing that more frequently. He wasn't one of her subordinates on the force; this was a partnership, and a struggle for independence and freedom from oppression.

"...Nzinga has *nothing* to do with this!"

"Hmph...I *bet*!"

"...For your information, I got the chance to meet Imakhu Senefra's *daughter* Nefertara last night! We both happen to be academics..."

"What...?!", she replies, stunned.

"...She came into town to surprise her mother! They hadn't seen each other for a while..."

"...Oh", was all Amirah could get out, after a long pause.

"...We were discussing her coming to Woodson-Rogers College to possibly do a speaking engagement. And for the record...Nzinga and I are just *friends* now."

Amirah now became embarrassed. She became angry with herself for letting her personal feelings of jealousy get in the way of her duties. She didn't want him to question her commitment to the movement, or her ability to handle her responsibilities as his partner. They had done a lot together; building up and expanding his network of contacts, informants, sympathizers, and clandestine supporters, practically building their own clandestine organization from scratch; the *F*reedman's *U*nderground *R*evolutionary *I*nitiative, or "F.U.R.I.". She had been able to help him to reboot, retool, and refine it's organizational structure, helping to make it untraceable by law enforcement. *This* is what she lived for, not the politics and corruption of the police force. She didn't know how she would be able to handle it, if he chose not to work with her anymore. "I'm sorry...", she says, "I shouldn't have come out my mouth like that".

"What's up? Talk to me."

"It's...nothing. Just...badge stuff..."

"Are you sure...?"

"Yeah, yeah...I'm just tired of it all..."

"Things aren't any better under Commissioner Seere...I know..."

"...He's just more sneaky and conniving with what he does. He and A. Simi are *perfect* for each other..."

"They, and others like them, will be brought down...trust and believe."

"I believe you...I always have."

Amirah flashes him a weary smile, trying to reassure him of her commitment. The Black Fist nods to her in return. He gets up, and heads toward the door, ready to go on patrol. "I should hit the streets...see what I can find...".

"Will you be taking the *Queen Amina* out for a spin...?"

"...Not tonight. I'll just travel through the rooftops...might have a better chance at seeing something from an elevated position."

"I'll track your signal, and provide support...", she says, heading for the computer station.

"...-Call it a night, Amirah! You're no good to me if you're all tired, and wound up."

"...What?!"

"...You've been working extended shifts. I need you well rested, and clear headed if you're going to help me crack this. Stand down...at least for tonight."

Amirah gives him a look, but doesn't say anything. She knew that her earlier outburst was the cause of this. Basically, he wanted some space from her, and having her in his ear all night wasn't going to relieve that. She didn't like it, but didn't half blame him. She sighs, nodding in return. "Okay".

She turns and exits, not even bothering to wait for a response. She doesn't wait, because she already knew that she wasn't going to get one. She wasn't going to get one, because she knew that he was already gone....

CHAPTER 6

Sekhmet Baset was making her way across the rooftops of Metro New Washington. She needed to reach her target before he left his location, looking to complete her mission. She moved swiftly and effortlessly through the night, doing Parkour across the rooftops of the buildings beneath her feet, acrobatically making her way across the roofs like the felines that she symbolically embodies. She flipped and jumped about, scaling the various walls and ledges like a human-sized cat. The light of the full moon added to the mystery of the night, casting spooky shadows about. The light of the moon seemed to invigorate her even more, giving her an added bounce to her step; channeling the energy of the neter Khonsu, neter of the moon, that energized her, pushing her forward to seek her target. She was singularly focused on her next target, and wasn't going to let anything come between her, and accomplishing her mission.

She stops just short of the Museum District, crouching down and surveying the scene. She sees the surrounding buildings that make up the museums of the city, taking in their stylized art deco designs. It is here that she was to seek her next target, an art smuggler, and have him eliminated. He was nothing more than a thief, and a black market dealer, stealing and selling ancient cultural artifacts to the highest bidder. It disgusted her how people like him were able to profit off of the misery of others, appropriating their culture for his own personal financial gain. She intently scans the streets, hoping to catch a glimpse of either her target, or his vehicle. *His luck...and his life...will end tonight*, she seethes in her mind, *no longer will he be able to profit off of the stolen cultures of others!*. Her eyes peer towards the street level, and she sees a recent model town car pulling up to the side entrance of the New Washington City Museum of Ancient History. Behind her helmet mask, her eyes narrow with intent. A sinister smile crosses her face. *Finally...*, she muses, now rising from her position.

"....-Ahem!"

Sekhmet Baset instantly turns around, her Khopesh sword immediately unsheathed from her back, getting into a combat stance. It thoroughly surprised her to have been snuck up upon like that; not many people had the skill set to do that, *especially* not against her. She is surprised to see The Black Fist just standing there, his arms folded across his chest, intently staring her down. It irritated her that he didn't seem the least bit intimidated by her. *Arrogant fool*, she thought, *He will soon meet his fate!*. "So...*you're* the one running around my city, causing problems that *I'm* getting blamed for...", he comments in his usual gravelly voice.

"<...-Do *not* interfere, or you *will* be slaughtered!>"

The Black Fist now becomes shocked, looking at her in utter surprise, momentarily loosing his composure.

"...You speak Medu Neter?!?!?"

Now it was Sekhmet Baset's turn to become shocked, and caught off guard. *He knows the language of the Mdw Ntr?!*, she thinks to herself. "<Who are you?! How do you know the language of the Mdw Ntr...?!>", her synthesized voice hisses at him.

"...-Whoa, whoa, whoa...slow down! I know what the language sounds like, but I don't speak it."

"Who are you...?", she responds after a moment, "...Why are you here?!"

"...The Black Fist. This is my home...I protect it."

"...Do *not* interfere! This does not concern you!"

"...-Murders in my city *do* concern me!"

"...I will *not* warn you again!", She hisses, "<Leave...*now!*>"

The Black Fist just simply pulls out his billy clubs, getting into a Maculelê fighting stance of his own. "I can't do that...", he replies, "So you either better be *really* skilled, or stand down-...". He barely finished his sentence, when she charges at him. The Black Fist is able to dodge her attack, just barely, and readies himself for combat. He combines the ends of his billy clubs, creating a staff, and readies himself for her oncoming attack.

The two clash on the rooftop, throwing everything into this battle. They dodge and attack, fiercely engaging each other, with neither of them backing down from the other. The Black Fist grabs a handful of his throwing darts, and flings them in Sekhmet Baset's directions, hoping to keep her off balance. She just counters by dodging his attack, and throwing her own arsenal of throwing knives. He barely dodges her volley, coming up in a fighting stance. *Damn...*, he thinks to himself, *she's really GOOD! I'll have to really be strategic to beat her....* There is a slight pause in their fight, as Sekhmet Baset also contemplates her next move. *His fighting skills are PHENOMENAL*, she thinks to herself, quite impressed, *he is definitely a worthy opponent! I will have to be careful with him....* She then puts her sword back into its sheath, and gets into an Ushat Ahad fighting stance, beckoning him to attack. The Black Fist pauses, surprised by this tactic of hers. *Is she serious...?!*, he thinks to himself, a mixture of confusion and annoyance.

"<...Come and face me, if you dare!>"
"...What the-...?!"
"<You dare to face me in combat...?! Then come face the consequences of your foolishness!>"

The Black Fist momentarily pauses, and then straightens up. He detaches his staff, and re-clips the two billy clubs back onto the back of his belt. He then gets into a Musangwe fighting stance. "Fine....", he growls, "...Have it your way...".

The two recommence with their battle. They throw their full skills into the fight, holding nothing back, wanting to prove to the other who is the superior fighter. They throw numerous combinations at each other, ducking, blocking, and parrying from each other. They then switch fighting styles against each other, trying to throw the other off balance, able to counter each others moves. Though very much heated, the battle is also starting to generate respect for the involved combatants, impressed with each others high level of fighting skill. They continue to clash with each other, throwing kicks, punches, and elbow strikes at each other, being able to block and counter each others attacks. Sekhmet Baset almost seemed to be *enjoying* this battle, this cat-and-mouse game of theirs; it'd been a long time since she'd fought a worthy opponent in battle, and relished this opportunity to really test her skills. The Black Fist, on the other hand, was growing concerned with the fight. During his travels and research, he had never encountered a fighter of this caliber. *She's really good*, he thinks, *I don't know if I'll be able to beat her if this drags on for much longer...*. Sekhmet Baset is able to back flip away from one of his attacks, and pulls out her whip. She swings it at him, trying to strike him with it. The Black Fist is able to see the attack coming, and barely dodges out of the way, rolling away from her. He finally comes to his feet, intently staring her down, pulling out his own whip and letting it unfurl. "We're going back to weapons now, eh...?", he seethes, "Afraid that you can't beat me by just using your hands...?".

Sekhmet Baset is about to respond when they hear a police chopper in the distance. They both turn towards the direction of the chopper, and see that it is heading towards their direction, its spotlight piercing the night sky. The Black Fist grimaces, annoyed to have their fight interrupted. The two combatants then turn to each other. Sekhmet Baset then places her hand on her heart, and bows to him.

"...Dua, Black Fist. <We will continue this at a later date.>"
"...Agreed! This ain't over!"
"<Until we meet again...>"

Sekhmet Baset takes off, making her way across the rooftops. The Black Fist briefly pauses, watching her as she leaves, feeling a bit saddened. As much as he didn't want to admit it, he actually *was* enjoying the fight. He rarely got the chance to fully test his fighting skills, other than the occasional scrape against Iggy Norance's people from The System. She really tested his training and fighting skills, taking to task everything that he has learned and written about. A slight smile crosses his face, now looking forward to his next encounter against her.

His attention is brought back by the sound of the approaching chopper. He turns towards the opposite direction, and make his own escape, disappearing into the darkness. He chose to save his animosity against the police for some other time; right now, he had to prepare himself for the next time he faced Sekhmet Baset. He was going to have to do some more intense training, and figure out a way to beat her in their next fight. He could tell that he wasn't facing her full potential; she had a more vicious and sadistic side to her, and that gave her that added edge in a fight. Would he be able to successfully challenge her, and win, if she were to tap into that side in their next fight...?

CHAPTER 7

Nyerere and Nefertara have been spending the day together, while Imakhu Senefra was going around the city, handling speaking engagements, and administering to followers. They were now eating at a vegan restaurant in southern Banneker Heights, enjoying each others' company. It felt good for Nyerere to be able to hang out with someone that was, not only the same age as he, but was also somebody that he felt was an intellectual equal. He didn't necessarily have a whole lot of close friends that he could relate to, considering his education and upbringing, and it felt good to be around someone he considered to be a kindred spirit. They'd spent most of the day talking academics, politics, the state of the movement, and the overall state of the community. They also shared about who were the biggest influences in their lives; academically, or otherwise. Of course, they both cited how their families have had such a huge impact on their lives. It felt good to Nyerere; he got the chance to really be himself, and *not* be consumed by the weight of the responsibilities of being The Black Fist.

"I really think that the students would enjoy you coming to the campus, and speaking to them, Nefertara..."
"...No need to try to sell me on a campus visit, brother. I'd be honored to come and speak."

"...Great! This would definitely make Dr. Oduno's day. He hasn't stopped celebrating getting *me* to work at the campus...hopefully hearing this news won't be too much for him..."

They both chuckle at his comment. Dr. Oduno had been working very hard to rebuild the college back up, and increase student enrollment. Being able to get Nyerere to come and teach, and bringing in some notable speakers and academics, has helped to inspire a slight growth in enrollment for the school, and to bring the school back to a sense of prominence. It was all about working together to help keep our institutions operational and afloat. If *we* don't work to maintain and support our own institutions, who will...?

"Don't worry about it, brother...I'm *more* than willing to work something out."

"...Great!"

"Actually...would you know if the campus has any part-time faculty positions open...?"

"...Really?!"

"...Yes. I would love to settle down somewhere...be closer to my mut...plant some roots..."

"I can definitely look into that for you. Dr. Oduno is *always* on the hunt for exceptional professors to come teach at the college..."

"...Dua ntchr, brother! You're quite an inspiration, Nyerere. I know how hard it can be...being a legacy and all..."

"...I know, right?"

"It's a great honor...and a heavy burden to carry at the same time."

"...*So*, true!", he replies, rolling his eyes a bit.

Nefertara laughs, and smiles at him. Nyerere joins in, but also sees something in her eyes as she looks at him. Their connection to each other seemed to be getting stronger by the minute, the longer that they were together. Her dark chocolate smile and chiseled features were drawing him in ever so deeply. There was just something about her that made her so...equal, almost *perfect*. He hadn't felt this intense a connection with anyone else before. He briefly shakes it off, trying to change the subject. He looks down at his phone, and checks the time. "Ugh...we better get going", he wearily sighs, "Shaka will have my head if we're late...".

"Sure, brother. We can always talk about this a little later. I wouldn't mind working closer with you, and your organization..."

"...I'd like that", he replies, smiling in return. He briefly pauses. "So shall we go...?"

"Yes...lets."

           *   *   *   *   *

The Sankofa-Ifa Community Center was abuzz with excitement. They were all in one of the larger dance rooms upstairs, packed full of people, save the small space allowed for the drummers and martial artists. When word got out that Nefertara was going to be gracing Shaka's class with her presence, the neighborhood youths came out of the woodwork to watch her in action, and see how the students stacked up against her. His classes were usually a private and quiet affair; mostly just filled with his students, and a few prospective future students watching on, contemplating on joining his class or not. Having an outside celebrity coming into the center always brought out the crowds, and this time was no different.

Nefertara catches one of his students with a foot sweep, knocking him off balance. She then grabs him by his sare, and tosses him onto the ground with a hip throw. The crowd cheers her fighting prowess, as she has taken down a number of Shaka's top students in a sparring match. The drummers stop playing as the match has ended. Nyerere, standing a little behind Shaka's position, snickers to himself, as yet *another* one of his students has fallen to Nefertara; seven in a row to be exact. The young man walks off, his pride wounded, trying to be consoled by his fellow students. Nefertara jovially turns to Shaka. "Malenga Shaka...dua for giving me this opportunity to spar with your mwanafundzi. It's been quite a while since I've had the opportunity to really train, and practice my skills...".

"Really...?", Nyerere snickers in a low voice, "...She could've fooled me..."

"...Shut up, Nyerere!", Shaka mutters back.

"I'm saying, though...they're getting clobbered by an out-of-practice *healer*..."

"...-It's *not* about winning! It's about gaining the experience of testing their skills..."

"What...like how to take a beating?", he snickers again.

"You know what, Nyerere...?", Shaka growls at him.

Nyerere just continues to snicker, enjoying this chance to get under Shaka's skin. Though things had gotten a bit better between the two of them, there was still that strain in their relationship; his hidden mistrust of Shaka, and his culpability in his parent's death. He was entrusted to protect them, and obviously hadn't lived up to that task. It's taken a very long time for Nyerere to find forgiveness for him, and it was something that he continued to struggle with.

Nefertara easily dispatches with yet another of Shaka's students. The crowd continues to applaud their appreciation of her skill. As the student slinks off, Nefertara turns to Shaka. "Malenga Shaka...I'm really enjoying this! Would you be interested in a sparring match...?", she asks. Shaka slightly blanches, being caught off guard by her request. She had easily dispatched some of his top students in his class; he didn't want to risk being embarrassed by a loss to Nefertara, and losing students because of it. If he were to lose any more students, that was a financial blow that the Center couldn't afford.

"Um...I would love to, sister, but...I'm nowhere near 100 percent..."

"Oh...?"

"...Yes, sister. Just getting over a cold, and recovering from injuries, and all..."

"...How sad. It would have been an honor for me to be able to say that I had the opportunity to spar with the great Shaka Mbari..."

"...Hopefully another time soon, sister."

Nyerere snickers, and playfully rolls his eyes. He knew that Shaka had backed down out of fear of losing to her. Nefertara looks past Shaka, and sees Nyerere. Her look of disappointment then turns into a sly smile. "Professor Lewis...", she calls to him, "I'm a *huge* fan of your work! Would you do me the honor of a sparring match? I would *love* to test out my skills against your theories in a combat situation...".

"Really...?", Nyerere responds, both surprised and amused.

"...Yes, brother! I would be honored to test out my limited skills against your vast wealth of knowledge..."

Nyerere knew that she was selling it a bit. She was basically calling him out, since Shaka had backed down. She playfully flashes him a sinister smile, daring him with her enchanting eyes. Nyerere just smiles at her in return.

"...Sure, why not?"

"...Dua, brother! I'd *love* to see how my skills stack up against yours..."

The room has become abuzz with excitement, the anticipation level higher than it was before. Even the elders had come out to watch their match against each other. Nyerere had changed his clothes into something more appropriate for sparring. The two are loosening their bodies up, getting ready for their sparring session. Many of the people in the audience have their phones out, ready to record their match, readying to post comments about it on social media. Nyerere and Nefertara both finish up, and nod their readiness to Shaka.

"Warriors...ready...!"

Nyerere and Nefertara bow to each other, and then get into a fighting stance of their chosen style, readying themselves to engage in combat. Shaka then turns to the drummers.

"...Drummers...ready...!"

The drummers position their drums, readying to beat out the rhythms of war for the two warriors before them. Angst and anticipation fills the room, the calm now coming before the storm.

"...Begin!"

The drummers start banging out a thunderous rhythm, and the two warriors engage each other. They spin, kick, punch, and flip about, showing the dearth of their fighting skills. The crowd continues to 'ooh' and 'ahh' as they parry and dodge, block and recover. They easily tease each other, testing each others' skills out, giving a good show, but not showing their full power and skills, outright. The crowd thoroughly enjoys the show, intoxicated by this display of skilled combat. Nyerere backs off a bit, looking for a way to breach Nefertara's defenses, and she presses her attack using Hikuta style. He now fights defensively, using Dambe style, blocking and dodging her attacks. Nefertara continues to smile at him, now pressing her own attack. They are both starting to enjoy the sparring session, getting the chance to really display their skills. The crowd in the room cheers them on, calling out to them, taking sides in the fight. Then something goes wrong...*very* wrong.

What the-...?!

Nefertara throws a strike at him, and it was almost as if it was telegraphed; he literally *saw* it coming before she threw it. He was able to easily avoid the blow, and throw her a bit off balance. *Is she trying to throw the fight...?*, he thinks to himself, *Why would she do that? She WANTED this match*. The look of shock and confusion on her face lets him know that she wasn't trying to throw the match. A determined look then registers on Nefertara's face, and she presses her attack again. This starts to confuse Nyerere even more, being able to read most of her attacks, before she even throws them.

No, she's not telegraphing her moves...I've SEEN this technique before...!

Nyerere then switches from defense to offense, pressing his own attack. He starts to switch styles on her, now using Kipura, trying to confuse her. He throws a patented spin-kick at her, and she surprisingly easily evades it. They both pause, surprised by this move.

What?!?! How did she even see that coming...?!

That was a move that he'd always used on the streets as The Black Fist. *Nobody* should know that technique unless they've battled him before, and survived. The crowd continues to cheer, totally oblivious to the dilemma brewing between the two combatants. Nyerere engages her one more time, trying to test out his theory that he hoped, that he *prayed* wouldn't be true. He attacks her using some more patented moves that he uses as The Black Fist, and she was able to read them all, and counter them.

Nefertara then immediately backs off, becoming completely shocked.

We've fought before...on the ROOF!

...It was YOU!

Both fighters stand there, completely shocked. This causes the crowd to look on in confusion, not knowing what was going on. "Nyerere, Nefertara...", Shaka calls out to them, "Is anything wrong...?". It surprised him the way that they'd both just abruptly stopped sparring. He was actually quite impressed, watching them battle each other, noticing how their skills had far surpassed his own, even at his peak. This abrupt stoppage in battle was quite confusing, though; they both looked as if they had just seen a ghost. Nefertara quickly bows down to Nyerere, officially ending the fight. "Dua for the match, brother...", she says quickly, "We must spar again, some other time...". She then quickly exits the room. Nyerere just watches Nefertara leave, still in shock, not really knowing what to say, or do. *This is just unreal...*, he thinks to himself, not wanting to believe it,*...this can't be...this just CAN'T be happening!* Some of the younger children in the crowd go up to Nyerere to congratulate him on his victory, cutting him off from going after her, oblivious to the way that he'd won. The crowd becomes baffled, and a bit deflated, murmuring their feelings of disappointment at how the match had ended. As the crowd begins to disperse and go about their separate ways, Tabula, Balogun, Waset, and Tehuti turn to Shaka, and sees him sharing that same look of utter confusion on his own face.

"What was *that* all about...?"

CHAPTER 8

Amirah was getting worried. She had returned to the hideout after her shift, and The Black Fist was nowhere to be found. She'd noticed that the *Queen Amina*, his specialized car, was missing from its parking spot in the basement of the building. With all of the construction that was going on in the increasingly gentrified city, it was getting harder for him to get around the city solely by the rooftops. She knew some officers that worked at the impound lot, and was able to get her hands on an old, unclaimed Jeep Grand Cherokee. They were able to get some brothers in F.U.R.I. that were mechanics to retro-fit the car for their purposes; making it bulletproof, painting it black, with RBG racing stripes on the sides, as well as painting the colors of the Black nationalist flag on the roof. It had the capability of being a mobile command unit, as well as a mode of transportation. He took the car out on occasion, sometimes even during foul weather. It soon became a favorite item of his to use. For whatever reason, he had turned the GPS off on it, and he wasn't answering his specialized cellphone. *What's going on...?*, she asked herself, *He usually doesn't go off grid like this.* The police blotter had been quiet; no more murders had happened since the last one a few days ago. Does this mean that the killer has accomplished their mission, and moved on...? Or, are they still searching out their next target, and laying in wait to eliminate them? She didn't like feeling helpless, and out of the loop; there was no reason for her to be shut out like this, not by

The Black Fist. Had her last outburst caused him to reconsider his partnership with her...?

Amirah tries to call him again, and receives no answer again. Since it was impossible to track their phones, she was back to square one. *Why is he doing this to me*, she asks herself, *I just hope that he's alright....*

*   *   *   *   *

Senefra was resting in the living room of the apartment that Waset and Tehuti had put her up in. She had been feeling quite drained lately, probably from all of the traveling that she'd been doing recently, and had dosed off. She had wrapped herself up in a long shawl, wearing an earthtone caftan, and was trying to enjoy some tea and music. Nefertara walks in, and sees her mother asleep on the couch. She affectionately smiles at her, wanting more than anything to crawl up under her, and feel her protective embrace. She felt confused, yet somewhat liberated in her recent discovery. She walks over to her mother, and gives her an affectionate hug from behind. This pulls Senefra out of her slumber, wiping her eyes. She sees her beloved daughter, and hugs her back.

"Hetepu, mut. I didn't mean to awaken you..."

"...It is alright, my dear child." She briefly pauses. "Your ka feels...disturbed."

"...It is alright, mut. A burden has actually been lifted..."

"...Yet, you still feel...troubled by it...?"

"...It was just...unexpected...that's all."

"The neteru will properly guide you. You are their vessel."

"...I know. Trust in them, and they will show me the way."

They both pause, and affectionately hug again. It had been way too long since they had been able to spend any real quality time together. Nefertara missed the warmth of her mother's embrace, the wisdom of her words, the caring touch of her hands. She was glad that her mother could be here for her during her time of need. "Let me brew you some more tea, mut", she says, "I have something that I want to talk to you about...".

"...Dua ntchr, Nefertara. You know that I'm always here for you..."

Nefertara is sitting on the roof, staring out into the night sky. Her heart is not as heavy as it once was earlier, glad to have been able to confide in her mother about her troubles. She missed being in Senefra's presence, and learning from her strength and wisdom. She was so grateful to her for everything that she had ever provided for her. She takes a deep breath, and lets out a weary sigh. "You might as well come out...I already know that you're there...", she calls out. She momentarily pauses, and then lets out another heavy sigh. She rises from her seated position, and turns around. "Please, come on out, Nyerere. I already know it's you...". The Black Fist finally emerges from

out of the shadows, coming out from behind one of the air conditioning ducts.

"...We need to talk!"

"...I know."

"Just...just who in the heck are you?! *What* are you...?!"

She briefly pauses. "I am a slayer of evil, and a protector of the innocent."

"...You! *You* killed those men!"

"...-I eliminated a threat to our people!", she responds, slightly annoyed.

"Does the Imakhu know about you doing this...?!"

"....Please! Who do you think *trained* me?"

"*What*...?!", he responds, utterly shocked.

"If it wasn't for her, I wouldn't even *be* here!"

"What kind of parent, in their right mind, would train their *own child* to be a killer?!"

"...-Leave my mut out of this", she warns, "She has *nothing* to do with this...!"

"...-She has *everything* to do with this, if you say that she trained you!"

"...-And what about *you*, Nyerere", Nefertara responds, now becoming annoyed, "Are

you the result of Africana P.R.I.D.E.'s efforts?"

"...-I *chose* this path! Nobody even knows about this...except for you."

"...-As did I! As I said...if it wasn't for my mut, I wouldn't even be here..."

"...Then make me understand...*why* would *any parent* teach their child to be an assassin?!"

Nefertara pauses, briefly looking away. She heavily sighs before she speaks, becoming slightly uncomfortable. "She's not my biological mother...".

"...*What*?!?!"

"My mut is not my birth mother."

"Wha-...??!! *How*?!"

Nefertara pauses, taking another breath. It seemed as if a burden was finally being lifted from her strong, proud shoulders. "I love her as if she *did* give birth to me. She's the only *real* mother that I've ever known...". "Please...", The Black Fist replies, taking steps towards her, lowering his sport goggles to expose his face, "Help me to understand....".

"My...my real family was damaged...broken. My dad was an abuser...broke up our family. He beat up my real mom, damaged her mind. He'd finally gotten himself locked up for it, but that forced us into the shelter system. My birth mom couldn't handle that, and had a mental break down. I ended up in the foster care system. I was eight..."

The Black Fist stands there, shocked. It was eerie how similar their lives were, being affected by tragedy at such an early age. He couldn't help but to empathize with her past tribulations.

"I ended up in a few foster homes that I hated. I ran away, and lived on the streets..."

"...Damn! That must have been rough..."

"...I was just a kid. I didn't really know how to survive on my own. Begging for scraps here and there, stealing food...? I lived like a wild animal...". She pauses, and then smiles. "...That's when I saw her. She was absolutely *beautiful*..."

"The Imahku...?"

"I was starving...dumpster diving for something to eat. She was out on the street, doing some shopping. She was just so proud and regal looking...the most beautiful woman I had ever seen." She briefly pauses. "I just *had* to follow her...find out more about her..."

"Did she know?"

"...Not at first. I followed her for a few blocks. She then stopped to greet a street vendor that she knew. She put down one of her bags of food, and started going through his merchandise..."

"What did you do...?"

She frowns, becoming sullen. "...I acted like a common savage. I ran over...knocked her over...grabbed her bag...and ran like hell."

The Black Fist pauses, shocked. It shocked him that she would act so desperately, even at such a young age. At the same time, he reflects on his own upbringing; had he not had the guidance and love of Tabula and Balogun, could *he* have ended up the same way...? How would his life have turned out, had they not taken him in after the murder of his parents? "What happened after that...?", he asks.

"Surprisingly, she chased after me...", she chuckles, her mood lightening, "She's a lot tougher than she looks. Chased me down for a good 2-3 blocks. I was crying when she finally caught me, pleading for her to not have me arrested." She continues to chuckle. "I was so messy, and pathetic looking. It must have broken her heart...she took pity on me..."

"...Oh?"

"...She took out a cloth, and started to wipe my face. She actually gave me a hug, and told me that it was alright. Mut took me back to that same vendor to pay for her stuff, holding my hand the whole way. She then took me to get something to eat. I told her everything..."

"How did she take it?"

"...She was heart broken. It hurt her to hear what had happened to me, and my family. She took me back to her place, gave me a bath and dinner, and a place to sleep. She then introduced me to her world, and I never wanted to leave after that. That's when she truly became my mut..."

"...Holy cow!"

"...She's the only woman to ever truly love me. I'm *honored* to be her daughter. I would do *anything* for her. That's why I chose this path..."

"I...I...understand..."

"...You do?"

"It's not so different from me...with how I lost my parents..."

"...And how you now do...this?"

"...Exactly."

"Me, too. I saw too many people being dismissive of my mut's efforts to heal our community...being predatory toward our own people. They would mercilessly terrorize our people...vandalize her temple...threaten others like us...like her..."

"Gee...why does *that* sound so familiar...", he sighs reminiscently.

"She saw something in me...I was meant to be more than just a priestess, or healer..."

"Enter your new incarnation...?"

"...Sekhmet Baset...slayer of evil, protector of the defenseless..."

"...And the Imakhu knows of this...?"

"...-She knows enough. When I was an initiate, she introduced me to some other priests that she knew that were involved in the warrior cults, and fighting arts..."

The Black Fist pauses. "Why tell me all of this...?"

"...Because I felt something when we fought...the first time. You weren't a dark presence; your ka was good. You channeled the energies of the neteru of war...Sekhmet...Apademak...Herukhuti...". She pauses. "You also have a protective nature about you...the essence of Heru...Baset..."

"...Our people need to be protected. I couldn't allow us to continue to operate in pure darkness."

"...Nor could I."

The Black Fist pauses. It felt good to be able to find a kindred spirit in the struggle. She was on the front lines of it, just like he was. Though he thought that her tactics were on the extreme side, he understood where she was coming from. He could identify with her; hell, *empathize* with her in this struggle. They followed similar paths, and their pasts were eerily identical.

"Dua, brother."

"...For what?"

"For listening to my history, and understanding."

"You're a sister in the struggle", he replies after a moment.

"Dua for your support. Most others would not understand..."

"I can't really be as judgmental, as you can see..."

"Will we see one another again...?"

"...I could always use another revolutionary associate", he replies, "This is a fairly large city..."

"...*Only* a revolutionary associate?", she asks, seductively smiling.

The Black Fist's eyes register surprise, being caught off guard by her comment. He then recovers, flashing a bit of a smile in return. "We'll see...", he returns, putting his sports goggles back on.

"Dua, brother. Enjoy the rest of your evening."

"Medase, sister. And you, as well."

"We can talk more tomorrow."

"I'd like that. Uhuru sase, sister..."

"Good night, brother."

The Black Fist disappears into the darkness. Nefertara starts to smile to herself. Perhaps she'd just found herself a permanent reason to stay in New Washington City...

CHAPTER 9

Amirah is at the precinct, sitting at her desk. She wasn't in the best of moods, having gotten very little sleep the night before. She hadn't heard from The Black Fist at all last night, and was growing very concerned. From what she knew, he hadn't scheduled any trips out of town, whether for academic, or crime fighting purposes. Though she was used to working late nights and going without sleep, she was in a grouchy mood. Most of her co-workers knew to stay out of her way, and she had to catch herself a few times from snapping at a few crime victims during interviews. It was making for a very crappy day at the job, one that she was beginning to immensely hate with a passion.

Her desk phone goes off. She groans, becoming annoyed at being imposed upon, yet again, and absently answers it. "Detective Umi...", she barks into the phone.

"I'm sorry...I should have called", a gravelly voice replies.

She pauses, shocked to hear his voice. "Hey...", she returns. She then crouches down a bit, lowering her voice, "Where the hell have you been?! I've been trying to reach you...".

"...I know. I...I had something that I had to sort out..."

"...Without *me*?"

"...It was something personal."

She briefly pauses. "Did...did I do something wrong...?", she finally asks. She had to know...

"...It's not you. I'd just discovered something, and I didn't know how to deal with it..."

"You wanna talk about it?"

"...Later. Off the phone."

"Oh...", was all she could say, feeling disappointment.

"...I still have trust in you, if that's what you're worried about. We're good."

"...Thanks", she says, smiling a bit, briefly pausing, "Ummm...it's...not just that..."

"...What, then?"

"Um...I'll-...we'll talk about it later."

"Fine. I'm late. Hit you later."

Click!

Amirah looks at the phone, somewhat surprised. She didn't expect him to end the call so abruptly. She just wearily sighs, and hangs up her own phone.

*   *   *   *   *

Ray Sysm was at the New Washington City Museum of Ancient History, sharing a luncheon with some of the other board members. These events were usually just good for a tax write off; they generally bored him to tears. He was there to help celebrate the addition of some new artifacts that the museum had just acquired; some hard-to-come-by relics had recently come into their possession, and been added to their ancient Egyptian exhibit. They had come across this rather shady fellow who had recently gotten these relics himself; no doubt pilfered from a 'legitimate' source, and bought on the black market. He really didn't care *how* they'd gottten it, just as long as he was able to get it himself, and show it off in one of his institutions. The local media outlets were all downstairs, waiting on them to make the announcement about the newest additions to their existing exhibit. He smiled to himself, imagining the additional revenue that would be generated by these new artifacts; increased admissions sales, more school trips, the upper crust crowd bringing their high-priced associates in for a visit. Yes, this was *definitely* much more financially rewarding that lobbyist work...

Nzinga and Malachi were waiting with the rest of the city's press core. Nzinga was skeptical of the whole event, having her own misgivings about Ray Sysm. She knew about his past as a lobbyist, and his financial support for the oppressive past administrations of the city, and federal government. His latest incarnation as a philanthropist was nothing more than a smokescreen, *especially* getting back into bed with his old buddy, Iggy Norance. They were two peas from the same pod, and were actually quite predictable, to the astute observer. Ray was the more public face of the two, while Iggy was more behind-the-scenes with his activity. She didn't trust either one of them, and was always suspicious of anything that they ever did. If it wasn't for the newest addition that they were adding to their Egyptian exhibit, Nzinga wouldn't even have bothered to come. She unfortunately had no choice, being there on assignment. At least she was able to get Malachi to agree to join her to cover this story. As she readied her audio recorder, and he his camera, they decided to take this time to swap some gossip before the unveiling of the new exhibit.

"Have you heard the recent news about our illustrious mayor...?"

"Ugh...", she groans, rolling her eyes, "What did he do *now*...?"

"...He's gonna run for a second term. Already waaaay ahead in the polls..."

"...Typical", she replies flatly.

"...Doesn't look like he's gonna face any real challengers, either..."

"...Nobody's got the clout. He's got *everybody* fooled."

"I'm surprised City Council President Bourgeiosie-Boulé isn't gonna try to run against him..."

"...She thought about it...for about *two seconds*. She's better off being his ally...its more beneficial to her, that way..."

"He's pissed off a lot of people, though..."

"...Not enough to make a difference. He's still got a lot of people bamboozled."

"Yeah...", Malachi wearily sighs, "...A lot of people are still pissed at us for some of our stories against him..."

"...At least *you* don't have to worry about getting emailed hate mail, because of it."

"You're not gonna run scared because of it, now, are you?"

"...Hah! Never that..", she sarcastically laughs, "I just wish that the people weren't so blind, and gullible to his b.s...."

"Hah! Now you're starting to sound like Nyerere..."

"Hey, when great minds think alike...."

"I'm sorry that things didn't work out between you two. He was cool peoples...and I think that he was really good for you..."

"Thanks, Mal."

"...He helped keep you grounded, and *not* to get yourself killed chasing down The Black Fist."

"You know, what...?", she laughs at him.

"...It's true!"

"Yeah...I guess he *did* help to give me some perspective..."

"Yeah...he gave you a reason to go *home* at night", he laughs.

Nzinga playfully punches him in the arm. Malachi just laughs in return, smiling at her. Nzinga just shakes her head, smiling in return. She had heard the rumors about A. Simi running for a second term. Though a lot of economic prosperity *did* come into the city under his administration, the question was actually; *who really* were the ones

that were actually benefiting from all of this prosperity? The incoming gentrifiers were

changing, not only the face of the city, but also it's very cultural essence and identity.

Not to mention, the police force hadn't gotten any kinder towards the indigenous

residents of the city; there was still *a lot* of over aggressive policing tactics, and abuse

going on, with much of it still being reported by the Griot's Call. It made her wearily

sigh at what *another* four years under his administration would be like, shuddering in

dread. As much as she loved working at the Griot's Call, and living in New Washington

City, she began to wonder if it was finally time that she moved on...?

CHAPTER 10

Amirah pulls into the basement of F.U.R.I.'s headquarters, parking her car. As she exits her car, she sees that the *Queen Amina* is parked back in its space. If he was off the premises, at least it was clear that he hadn't taken the car. She makes her way over to the service elevator, closes it's gate, and pushes the button to go up to the top floor. She wearily sighs to herself, hoping to have a serious talk with The Black Fist. It was getting harder for her to restrain herself, and deal with all of the crap at the precinct at the same time. Perhaps it finally *was* time for her to turn in her badge? Her job wasn't fulfilling her, not in the least, and running F.U.R.I. was something that she could see herself doing for the rest of her life. The evil that existed out there needed to be challenged head on, and consistently. She utterly despised the likes of Iggy Norance, Ray Sysm, Mayor A. Simi Leishon-Intergration, and Commissioner Ovie Seere; how they've oppressed the communities of the city and beyond, with their financial and political influences; their private security force (really, an army) The System, who they used to strong-arm their influence over others, if money didn't work. Plus, she wanted nothing more than to be by Nyerere/The Black Fist's side. It was all becoming overwhelming, and she really needed someone to talk to, to get all of this off her chest.

The elevator finally comes to a stop at the top floor. Amirah opens the gate, and absently walks out, not really paying attention to her surroundings. All of a sudden, her senses start screaming for her attention, urging her to action.

Danger...!

Amirah looks up, and sees a figure clad in white and black, wearing a black cat-headed helmet mask, turning in her direction. *What the hell-...?!*, she mentally screams. She becomes shocked, and pulls out her gun. Sekhmet Baset also reacts, diving onto the floor, rolling, and coming up on one knee, ready to throw a barrage of throwing knives at her. Amirah aims her gun, ready to fire...

"...-Freeze!"

Three Black Star throwing stars flies between the two female combatants, startling the both of them, momentarily. The Black Fist jumps in between the two of them, unmasked, his gloved hands held up in front of both of them. He looks between the two women, trying to reply in a calm voice.

"...-Stand down! Both of you...*stand down!*"
"What the *hell*, Fist...?!?!", Amirah yells, trying to angle her gun for a shot.
"...-Stand down! I'll explain everything!"

They all pause for what felt like hours. Amirah looks The Black Fist in his eyes, looking

for reassurance. He nods to Amirah, and then she begrudgingly lowers her weapon, not

taking her eyes off of the intruder. The Black Fist then turns to Sekhmet Baset, still on

one knee, her throwing knives still in hand, ready to let loose her volley. He sternly

looks at her, determined to diffuse the situation.

"...-Lower your weapons! She's with me."

"Who is she?!", her synthesized voice seethes.

"...We're comrades...partners. I trust her with my life. Now, stand...*down*!"

Sekhmet Baset pauses, then puts her knives away. Even through the mask, Amirah

could feel her eyes intently sizing her up. Sekhmet Baset then rises, and Amirah notices

that she's actually female. Amirah then takes a weary breath, and holsters her gun. The

Black Fist finally lowers his arms, and turns to Amirah. He sees that she's giving him a

dirty look, not one that's undeserved.

"...Noooot exactly the way that I wanted to introduce you guys..."

"Who's your friend...?", she snidely asks, "I thought that the clubhouse was private...?"

"Amirah...this is Sekhmet Baset. Sekhmet...this is Detective Amirah Umi."

The two women icily nod to each other, their mistrust for each other growing by the second. Or, was it something *else* that was causing the temperature in the room to drop tremendously...?

"Welcome to the revolution...", he mutters to himself, heading over to the computer station. The two women continue to icily stare each other down, their mistrust for each other rising. "I thought that we were supposed to be working on a case...?", Amirah adamantly responds, still not taking her eyes off of Sekhmet Baset, "...But you're giving tours of F.U.R.I.'s headquarters, instead...*unmasked*?!".

"...The case has been solved."
"...What?!", Amirah replies, shocked, turning to him.
"...I found out who was taking out those people."
"What?! *Who*?!?!"
"...That would be me", Sekhmet Baset responds.
"...*What*?!?!", Amirah responds, turning to her in shock.
"...-They posed a threat to our people, and I *eliminated* that threat!"

Amirah turns to The Black Fist, looking at him, shocked and incredulous. The Black Fist lets out a weary breath, and swivels his chair around to face her. Her piercing, judging eyes didn't seem to be fazing him. "She *murdered* those people...and then, you just *invite* her in?!", she asks, exasperated.

"...-*Like* I said...", he returns, his eyebrows furrowing, "...They were *racists*! I'm *not* gonna lose any sleep over their passing."

"...That's *not* how we operate, Fist!"

"...-Since when, and says *who*?! Maybe we *should* operate that way..."

"*What*?!?!"

"...-They have *a history* of eliminating our leaders, and warriors. I know that for a fact, *personally*...do you?!"

She pauses, looking at him irate. "Don't talk down to me like I haven't contributed, Fist!"

"...You're still thinking like a cop. This is a *war*! Our tactics need to change!"

"Hey...*you're* the one that want me to be an infiltrator, *remember*?!"

He shoots her an annoyed, sarcastic look. This had been an issue brewing with her, and between the two of them, for quite some time. She had been growing more and more dissatisfied with her life on the police force, but had access to information that was vital to their plans, and helped them to keep track of the moves of the powers-that-be. "You have access to information that we need! Everybody plays their role-...", he sternly says.

"...-We have *other* infiltrators and sympathizers within the department who can get access to that *same* information! You *don't* need *me* specifically to access it!"

"Maybe so...but these soft tactics that we've been using hasn't been hindering them one bit! I don't remember anybody ever *negotiating* their way to freedom!"

"...-Don't give me that warrior crap, Fist! I'm just as willing to put my life on the line for the cause as *you* are!"

"...These guys need to be *destroyed*! Are you in, or, are you out?!"

"Are you *serious*...?!", Amirah nearly shrieks, "I've given up the last four years of my life-...!"

"...-And I've given up *thirty-one*!"

Amirah pauses, looking at him, both shocked and hurt by his response. She thought that he'd had more respect for her than that, that she had earned better over the years. She was hoping that she hadn't been letting her personal feelings for him cloud her judgment about their operational relationship. She was committed to be by his side, through any and everything, fighting until the bitter end. Apparently, he had found a replacement for her, in more ways than one. The Black Fist sees the hurt look on her face, and takes a heavy breath, regretting what he'd said, trying to start over...

"Well...I guess this is no longer a *partnership*..."

"Look, Amirah-..."

"...-Hey...it's fine by me...", she says, turning and walking away, trying to hide her cracking voice, "...It'd be nice to actually have a fucking life for once..."

"Amirah-..."

"...-Enjoy the revolution...*without* me!"

She heads towards the elevator, trying to hide the tears that were ready to stream down her face. "Why'd I have to fall for a fucking revolutionary...?!", she asks herself. She slams the gate to the elevator, and pushes the button for the ground floor. The car begins to descend towards the basement, with Amirah disappearing from sight.

The Black Fist watches her leave, shocked by her words. Amirah probably hadn't expected to have said that as loudly as she did, nor for him to have heard it. He stands there, stunned. He knew that there had been some tension brewing between the two of them, but he didn't really know how deep it went. There were many times when they had felt so close, but also had times of intense friction. *Was THAT the cause of all of this, all along...?*, he thinks to himself. As he stands there lost in thought, Sekhmet Baset watches him, trying to read his mood. "I...apologize", she finally responds, "I didn't mean to cause you any troubles, brother. I did not know that the two of you were...involved". He turns to her, a shocked look now covering his face. He briefly pauses, and then turns away, trying to gather himself.

"It's okay. It's...complicated."

"...So I see."

"We'd basically built F.U.R.I. together, from scratch..."

"...An intelligent sister-warrior, then", she replies, now gaining respect for Amirah.

"...Apparently, one that I haven't properly appreciated."

"We are warriors", she concedes, "But, sometimes, we need to see more than just the battle ahead..."

"...True."

He briefly pauses, taking a weary breath. He then goes to grab his crown, and sports goggles. "I need some air...", he says, "...Come on".

"Where are we going...?"

"...Going on patrol. Plus, there are some other associates in the network that I want to introduce you to."

"...Then, please...lead the way, brother."

He dons his headgear, and they head out onto the roof. As they go about, traveling across the roofs using Parkour, The Black Fist contemplates how he's going to convince Amirah to remain in the revolutionary fold, and earn her forgiveness. She is a strong and dedicated sister, and deserved to be treated with the utmost respect. He probably couldn't have achieved *any* of his goals for F.U.R.I. without her, and she had always been by his side, practically since the very beginning. He now had to figure out how he was going to earn back her trust and friendship, and remain a part of the movement.

Yes, things were complicated indeed...

CHAPTER 11

Mayor A. Simi Leishon-Integration is at City Hall, finishing up a meeting with his Schools Chancellor, Edwina "Miss Eddy" Yuecation. She was the lone holdover from the previous administration of Mayor Tom Token, and had been the head of New Washington City's school system for a number of years. There were those from the teacher's union and parents associations that were *very* unhappy with her tenure as chancellor, and were calling for her removal from her post. They didn't like how the educational system had become so testcentric, not to mention, the closing of many of the city's schools over the years. He wanted to reassure her that he had the utmost confidence in her, and that she still had a place in his administration. He didn't want any loose ends dangling during his reelection campaign, and to shore up his support base. A. Simi knew that he had the continued backing of Mr. Iggy Norance, and his partner Ray Sysm, who continued to be big contributors to his reelection campaign. Many of the power players in the city and beyond still supported him unconditionally; he'd brought them a lot of prosperity during his short time in office. Petite let him know that she would support his reelection bid, and would work her magic within the City Council to gain him the support that he needed to win, unopposed. Though there were a few city council members that he'd been at odds with, they generally let him reign over the city as he pleased, unopposed. "Trust me, Miss Eddy..." he soothingly replies, "You have *nothing* to worry about. You're not going anywhere. I have the utmost faith in you...".

"...Good", Miss Eddy says, "As long as I know that I still have *your* support..."

"People like to complain, but do nothing about changing their situation. You're doing a great job..."

"...Thank you, Mr. Mayor."

"The union people just want to squeeze us for more money, and earn a paycheck while doing nothing. They've brought nothing to the table, except a lot of hot air..."

"...Yes. I can't help it if they send their damaged kids to our schools, unprepared..."

"...Nobody wants to accept responsibility anymore, these days..."

"No, Mr. Mayor...nowadays, they don't..."

They both briefly pause. They continue on with their conversation for a bit more, and then Miss Eddy Yuecation finally leaves. He let her know that her job was secure, and she let him know that he had her unconditional support. A. Simi smiles to himself, feeling that another landslide victory was in his political future. His attention is drawn away, when his intercom buzzes for his attention. He presses the button, responding to his secretary. "Yes...?".

"Mayor Leishon-Integration...Governor Wyatt Supremacy is on the phone..."

"...Really?!", he responds, shocked.

"Yes, sir."

"Patch him through..."

A. Simi turns off the intercom, and picks up his desk phone. He was quite surprised to be hearing from the governor. They'd had quite the cordial relationship during his time in office, and seemed to get along pretty well with each other. They'd done quite a bit together to bring prosperity to both the city, and the state. "Governor Supremacy...", A. Simi jovially replies, "How are things with you, Wyatt?".

"...I can't complain, A. Simi. How are things in my city?"

"...As well as can be expected. These are interesting, and prosperous times."

"That, they are, A. Simi...that, they are."

"I couldn't have done it without your support..."

"...You scratch my back, I scratch yours."

"...It's the only way to do business."

"I hear that you're running for reelection...?"

"Yes, sir. That is correct."

"Congratulations! I know that it's in the bag."

"Well...it's not official yet, but-..."

"...-Trust me, you have *nothing* to worry about. You come highly recommended. A lot of people have your back."

"That's good to know, sir. I'm glad that I have your support."

"Well, our State A.G. speaks *very* highly of you, and I totally trust his judgment."

A. Simi had to smile at that. After his first year in office, Governor Supremacy's Attorney General decided to step down, and D.A. Wyatt Privilege was selected by the governor to take over the post. He gladly jumped at the chance to work with the real political powers that be, and be a big part of the governor's administration. When Privilege left, his E.A.D.A Gaitlin "Gait" Keeper stepped in to take his place. She's been loyally serving A. Simi ever since, and he was considering making her his permanent District Attorney once he's reelected. "He's a smart man...", A. Simi says, "...He keeps good company".

"...I trust that our mutual interests will still continue to be looked out for?"

"But, of course."

"...Good! As long as things are maintained as they are, we'll *all* benefit from this."

"...As it's always been."

"Good. I'm glad that we understand each other."

"Thank you, Governor Supremacy."

"Good luck, A. Simi. And just to let you know...you have my support."

"...That's good to know, Governor Supremacy."

They chit chat for a few more minutes, and then hang up. This draws an even bigger smile out of A. Simi. Yes...life at the top was good.

CHAPTER 12

Sekhmet Baset's head was spinning. She was amazed at all that Amirah and Nyerere had been able to build into F.U.R.I., in such a short amount of time; alternate safe houses, emergency medical stations in case of sickness or injury, their web of infiltrators and informants, their web of technicians, etc. They even had other 'revolutionary associates' that he'd met during his travels locally and abroad, that he occasionally works with. It made her want to work more closely with The Black Fist, and be a permanent member of their movement. The access to their information network alone was enticement enough to get her to want to join up. No longer would she have to tackle these issues alone; there was an entire network of dedicated brothers and sisters working to challenge and dismantle this system of oppression. She began to feel more alive, now knowing that there was help out there, if she ever needed it, to complete her mission. Not only did she have access to assistance locally, there were brothers and sisters ready to help her throughout the diaspora, across the world.

Sekhmet Baset and The Black Fist had parted ways; he'd discontinued with his patrols, calling it a night, while she felt the need to continue on. She was glad to see Nyerere was coming around to her way of thinking, as far as handling their enemies were concerned. At the same time, she felt partially responsible for the friction that was now brewing between he and Amirah. Any woman who was able to accomplish what Amirah had with building this organization the way she did, deserved her utmost respect. *Things will work themselves out,* she thought to herself. She didn't know Amirah very well, nor for very long, but from what Nyerere had told her, she was beginning to have great respect for her.

She'd made her way back to Downtown New Washington City, tracking down her lost target. He had foolishly stayed in the city, hoping to score some more financial dividends from other prospective clients. He'd also foolishly wanted to indulge himself with some local prostitutes, as a reward for his recent financial windfall. She'd tracked him down to a local hotel near the Museum District, relieving himself with a local sex worker. Literally catching him with his pants down, Sehkmet Baset had him tied up in a chair, his mouth gagged. She pulls out her Khopesh sword, skillfully waving it in front of his frightened face. "Now...", she hisses at him, "Let's get back to those artifacts you sold...".

*   *   *   *   *

Ovie was sitting in his office, going over some files. Things had been quiet recently on the streets, as far as the killings were concerned, but he still had other issues to deal with. He still had the headache of dealing with the local activist community, and the local Black press breathing down his neck. It made him long for the days when he was running The System for Mr. Norance. *Oh well...*, he sighs to himself, *That's what happens when he feels like you didn't do your job. You pay the consequences....* He briefly pauses, rubbing his eyes. His desk intercom goes off, alerting him to his secretary's presence. "Yes...?", Ovie answers.

"Commissioner Seere...former Commissioner Brutus is here to see you..."

Ovie pauses, quite surprised. He'd always respected the man, though he didn't get the chance to work with him much, before. "Please...send him in", he replies. After a few moments, the doors open, and Brutality enters into the office. Ovie rises, and extends his hand to him, a slight smile coming across his face. "Commissioner...!", Ovie replies, "It's good to see you again...".

"...Commissioner. Likewise."

"So...what brings you around your old office?"

"...Just a bit of follow up."

"Ah...I see."

"Mr. Norance is...unhappy...about recent events."

"...Understandable. Neither am I."

"I'm looking into some leads. And...he wants some assurances that something like this won't happen again."

"...Not if I can help it!"

"...Exactly as I told him."

"But...he still wants some assurances, right?"

"...Exactly."

"Have you been able to find out anything on your end, with your resources?"

Brutality briefly pauses, stewing in his own annoyance. "No...we haven't". Ovie pauses, not really the answer that he was hoping to hear from his replacement. "Well...", he responds, "We'll keep investigating".

"...And I'll see what we can do on my end."

"Rest assured...we *will* find this person, and stop them!"

"I have no doubt, Commissioner."

"Thanks", Ovie says, "I really appreciate the support."

"I've held your spot...I know what it's like...what you go through, and have to deal with..."

"Not many understand, eh?"

"...Nope. Not unless you've worn a badge, or have held this job." Brutality pauses, then flashes him a reassuring grin. "For what it's worth...I have complete faith in you, that you'll do a good job."

"...Thanks, Joseph. It's much appreciated."

"Makes you long for the old days, don't it?"

"...Hah! Always. It's not so bad, though..."

"The new administration treating you good?"

"I can't complain. A. Simi has my back, so that helps a lot..."

"...At least he's better than that good-for-nothing Mayor Token. He was a pain in my ass!"

"...At least I'm lucky in that regard. The mayor and his people back me up pretty good, I'd say..."

A. Simi's administration was very much pro-police. Acting-D.A. Gaitlin "Gait" Keeper never sought to prosecute any of his people for any infractions against the police department, picking up where her former boss left off. Not to mention, he also had the full support of the mayor, and his Deputy Mayor Orrin "Orr" Reo, a former A.D.A, himself. These were definitely better times for the police department. It made Brutality feel a bit of jealously for him; if he'd had the free reign now being given to Ovie while *he* was still Commissioner, who knows how much influence he'd be able to exert on the streets? *Oh well...*, he thinks to himself, *It's HIS headache to deal with, not mine. Things are going fine for right now; who's to say how things will go, after a major incident happens?* With the activist community, not to mention The Black Fist, always causing some sort of trouble, things are bound to go wrong. Brutality shakes his head clear, and readies himself to leave. "We'll keep you in the loop as to our progress...", he

says.

"...And we'll do the same on our end."

"Glad that we had this talk, Commissioner."

"...Likewise. You're always welcome to stop by any time."

"Thank you, Commissioner."

"...You're welcome, Commissioner."

The two men shake, and after a slight pause, Joseph turns, and exits his old office.

Waves of nostalgia start to hit him as he leaves. He didn't necessarily want to leave

office, but when Iggy made him the offer to come and work for him, he could hardly

refuse. Working for a man of Iggy's stature was a no-brainer; he's not the type of person

that you say 'no' to. Plus, he has more free reign to do what he wants with his agents

working for him in The System; more than he *ever* could in the police department. The

System was a well oiled machine, and had unlimited powers, all at his disposal.

Brutality loved the department, but loved the power of The System even more. As he

enters the elevator, Brutality smiles to himself. Perhaps working in the private sector

wasn't so bad after all...?

CHAPTER 13

Amirah was not in the best of moods when she showed up for the call. Having walked away from F.U.R.I., her nights were now back open, and she tried to fill them up by catching up on some much needed sleep. But of course, with crime in New Washington City's streets being the way it is, she couldn't count too much on having any quiet evenings. She shows up at the seedy motel right outside of the city's Museum District, and makes her way upstairs to the room of the latest crime victim. At first, Amirah was surprised that a motel such as this one still existed in the city; they had done a lot of gentrification in the city, and small motels and hotels such as this one were usually swallowed up in the process. Secondly, she was surprised to see the other detectives that had called for her to be on the scene. She walks into the room, and sees his familiar pale face turning to her, and smiling.

"Hey Amirah."

"...Detective Brown! John!"

The two greet each other warmly, but professionally. Since her association with The Black Fist, Amirah had kept her encounters with other cops to a minimum. She'd always respected John, though, and was glad to hear when he'd taken the exam for detective, and had passed. "It's good to see ya", she replies.

"...Same, here."

"What have you got?"

"...Another body. I think that it's a part of that case you've been working on..."

"Oh...?"

"...He fits the M.O. you're looking for", a female voice pipes from off to the side.

They both turn to a young female, now crouched over the body. She sports barely shoulder-length brown hair, and well tanned southern European features. Her elfin face finally turns to them, a bit of excitement gleaming in her eyes. Amirah looks at her with a bit of surprise, vaguely remembering her after John's promotion. "Amirah...you remember my partner, Abigail Lishonist, right?", he asks. She stands up, now a full blown smile, and sticks out her hand. "Abbey's fine", she says, "Heard a lot of good things about you from John, here...".

"Thanks. He's helped me out a few times. Was glad to hear when he got his gold shield..."

"He's a good teacher, and partner as well."

"What can I say...?", John says, smiling at Amirah, "I learned from working with the best."

Amirah lets an embarrassed smile slip out. They then all turn their attention to the body in front of them. He was bound to the room's chair, which was now lying backwards on the floor of the room. He had obviously been beaten and tortured; his body was covered in bruises, and dried blood was on his underclothes. "What's his connection to my murders...?", Amirah asks.

"...He's an antiquities dealer", Abbey replies, "Apparently, the question is...*how* he gets those items is the problem."

"Stolen...?", Amirah asks.

"That's the rumor", John says, "He'd just delivered some stuff to the museum out here just the other day..."

"The one that Ray Sysm sits on the board of...?!", Amirah asks, slightly shocked.

"...That's the one", Abbey replies.

Amirah pauses. Her first instinct was to excuse herself, and make a secret call to The Black Fist, and fill him in on the news. After a second thought, she thought better of it, reasoning that he'd probably ordered his murder, now aligning himself to Sekhmet Baset's ideological tactics. She lets out a sigh, and moves in closer to inspect the body herself. From what she'd seen at the other crime scenes, it definitely did fit Sekhmet's M.O., as far as viciousness was concerned. "Brutal...", Amirah says.

"What's that old saying...", Abbey asks, "...Death by one thousand cuts...?"

"...And a few knuckle tattoos to boot."

"...As well as a *heel* tattoo...an *elbow* tattoo...probably a knee as well...", John comments.

"Should we report in to the brass...?" Abbey asks, "...Or, should we call in a special favor to a friend?"

Amirah turns to her, raising her eyebrow. Both Abbey Lishonist and John Brown were sympathizers, and had the vaguest association with F.U.R.I. They supported the movement, and did what they could to assist with information and resources. Amirah pauses, and takes a weary breath. "He might be a little indisposed right now...", she wearily responds.

"You think so...?"

"This is a big city...there's a lot going on."

"...More important than murder?!"

"...-We have murders *every* night", Amirah responds, slightly snapping, "Is he supposed to solve every single one?! Or, can we do our fucking jobs...?"

"Whoa! Easy, Amirah...", John says, a little shocked, "We're all on the same side here..."

Amirah pauses, taking a breath. She was letting her anger with Nyerere get the better of her, and was taking it out on others. Despite being a rookie detective, Abbey meant no harm with her statement. She wasn't like the other officers on the force, which was why Amirah had approached her as a sympathizer to F.U.R.I.'s cause. "I'm sorry, Abbey...", Amirah says, "I didn't mean to bite your head off...".

"...No offense, taken."

"...It's just been one of those weeks..."

"We get it...", John says, "...This is a tough case."

"...Among other things", Amirah mutters, more to herself.

"I guess we can't expect our friend to solve *all* of our problems...", Abbey says.

"...That's what they have *us*, for", Amirah responds.

Amirah wearily sighs. She beings to exit. "Let me know when you've got something...", she says, "...And get the forensics team to give us the works". "You've got it, Detective...", John returns. Amirah exits the room, and makes her way back downstairs to her car. She was getting a creepy feeling, not liking how this was going. Her mind focused back on her last encounter with Nyerere at the hideout. Was he going to start wantonly attacking Iggy Norance and their ilk? Will he start picking off their operatives and supporters, like a hit list? She liked and respected the fact that if he did take a life, it was always only in self defense. Will he reject that stance, and now call for all out bloody war? It saddened her deeply, feeling like she was now possibly losing

him in more ways than one...

CHAPTER 14

Nyerere was not in the best of moods. He was at the Sankofa-Ifa Community Center, spending some time with the elders, finally showing his face out in public, and getting some extra practice time in. He'd read the recent headlines of the Griot's Call, and immediately grew concerned, and increasingly agitated. Mayor Leishon-Integration's reelection campaign was not only going well, but was also growing really strong. He hated that man with a passion, and couldn't understand why he had the level of support that he did among both the politicians, and the people. His entire administration was full of nothing more than neocolonialists in blackface, who had done *nothing* for the benefit of the people of the city. The support that he was receiving from Iggy Norance, Ray Sysm, and Governor Wyatt Supremacy not only made him a political powerhouse, it also made him extremely dangerous, and a serious threat. But, what was *really* weighing heavily on his mind, was the report of yet *another* murder in the city. He had no doubt in his mind that Nefertara was behind it, and thought that this particular murder was uncalled for. Her other targets, he understood; they were evil men that had done many evil deeds. This antiques dealer, on the other hand, was probably nothing more than a petty thief; not really deserving to have his life taken. He agreed with her about taking a harder stance against their enemies, not being so merciful to those who didn't deserve it; it was *justice* that they were after. But...victims such as this antiquities dealer...? It was uncalled for, in his opinion. He deserved incarceration at the most, not death. Nyerere definitely felt that he needed to talk to Nefertara about this latest action...

Nyerere was in one of the empty dance rooms, practicing. It actually felt good to be out of F.U.R.I.'s headquarters, and be around other people. Leading a double life definitely had it's drawbacks; he always had to be careful about what he said, and how he acted around people. At the same time, constantly being by himself in that warehouse can wear on your nerves, and drive you a little batty. He was taking his recent frustrations out on his imaginary opponent, throwing kicking and punching combinations about, switching styles, letting out all of his anger, and agitation. It seemed like many things were starting to pile up on him all at once; Mayor Leishon-Integration and the political landscape, the police force, The System, his relationship woes, and now his issues with Amirah. If there was *ever* a time when he needed to open up a can of whup ass on a miscreant to relieve some stress....

Nyerere finishes up, and lets out a frustrated breath. He didn't feel any better after his workout; he just felt even more frustrated than before. He was beginning to get that same feeling as before; having the weight of the world on his shoulders. Before, he at least would have Amirah to talk to about having days like this; that wasn't an option that he had, right now. It made him miss and appreciate her even more, and really regret the

falling out that they'd had. He must have been radiating intense disturbed energy,
because Mama Tabula addresses him from the door.

"Are you okay, Nyerere...?"

Nyerere turns to her, caught off guard. His mind and senses must have *really* been
preoccupied if he couldn't sense her standing there. "Mama Tabula...", he replies,
shocked, "...How long have you been standing there?".

"...Not long. But, long enough to see that something's really bothering you."
"...It it *that* obvious?"
"...To those of us that really care about you, yes."

Nyerere wearily sighs. He drops to the floor, crossing his legs. Tabula walks in, and
joins him, kneeling onto the floor as well. "Tell me, baby...", she asks, "What's wrong,
Nyerere...?".

"Thing are better than they were before, but...", he pauses, "...You ever feel like the
weight of the world is on your shoulders?"
"...Occasionally. The struggle can get overwhelming at times..."
"...*Tell* me about it!"

"You've been able to do a lot, Nyerere. We've *all* been able to accomplish a lot these last few years, despite a lot of the resistance that we've faced..."

"It never feels like it's enough..."

"...It never does."

"Its just...it feels like everything is coming down on me all at once..."

"...Like, what? *For* what? With as much as you've done...*nobody* should be giving you any guff about what you should be doing. That's why Balogun and I raised you the way we did...we wanted you to find *your own* path...and you have."

"Sometimes...I just feel....lost."

"Really?"

"I don't know...I just see these two paths. They're quite different from each other...and now...I don't know which one to take..."

"Search your heart...and seek guidance from your elders, and ancestors. Spirit will never steer you wrong."

"I know, I know. My *head* knows that...but, my heart..."

Tabula pauses, and slowly smiles at him. She reaches out, and strokes his face. "You *don't* need to be your parents", she says to him, "Be *your own* person. That's all you need to be". Nyerere returns a slight smile to her. "Thanks, Mama Tabula", he says in return. They give each other a loving embrace, Nyerere's spirits now lifting. It always felt good for him to talk to his elders, and be guided by their wisdom and experience. "Come on...", Tabula says, rising from her position, "I should have some leftover Joloff rice, and oxtails in the fridge downstairs". Nyerere's face lights up, and he immediately rises after her. "Now you're talking my language!", he excitedly returns. Tabula just lets out a chuckle, and takes his hand. They help each other up, and leave out of the dance room. Tabula always did know what it took to cheer him up, and wanted to help raise his spirits. He had seemed so down today, not like his usual jovial self. His mood had improved greatly over the last few years, and she didn't want him to backslide back into his previous dark mood of years before. That darkness nearly drove him away, and out of their lives. Under no circumstances did she want him to return to those times, and lose him forever. *I'll have to watch him more carefully*, she thinks to herself. The *last* thing that they needed was to lose a young warrior such as Nyerere from their ranks. Not only was he an up-and-coming force to be reckoned with in the movement, but she couldn't bear to lose her adoptive child. She wanted to be able to keep him as close to her as she could, for *as long* as she could. *Perhaps I could enlist the help of Nefertara...?*, she thinks to herself, *they seem to really like each other*. As they head to the kitchen to enjoy a meal together, she begins to make plans of her own...

CHAPTER 15

Nefertara was in the apartment, taking the time to meditate. Imakhu Senefra was out taking care of some speaking engagements, so she'd decided to take this time to focus her energies. The smells of sage and frankincense fills the air, as she also surrounds herself with candles. She breaths in deeply, trying to reach a higher spiritual plane, trying to find her center. She has a CD playing music in the background, the sounds of chanting and singing in the ancient language filling the air, reverberating throughout the apartment. She sends mental messages out to the neteru that she prays to, seeking their wisdom, guidance, and energy...looking for their assistance to propel her toward her goals, and assist her in her mission. They had never steered her wrong before, and she knew that they wouldn't steer her wrong now. Nefertara was hoping to realize her options, to figure out which path to travel. She respected Nyerere, and was starting to grow very fond of him, being such a kindred spirit with an eerily similar history. At the same time, the path that he traveled was a bit restrictive; your enemies needed to be purged and eliminated. They cannot be allowed to grow powerful; you must keep them in a weakened state. She also wanted to be closer to her mut, and find a place where she can settle down, and plant some roots. She needed guidance as per her next step, and was hoping that the neteru would be able to provide her with some answers, and direction.

She feels her body radiating with energy, surging with a power that she's never felt before. She knew that it had to be the hand of the neteru channeling through her, guiding her to the right path that she was seeking. She opens her eyes, now feeling renewed and refreshed, with a renewed sense of purpose. She knew what her next mission was to be, and needed to prepare herself for it. She takes a deep breath, and rises, stripping off her robes, showing off her well toned, smooth, muscular, dark chocolate body. She heads towards the bathroom, and runs a bath for herself, ready to cleanse herself before commencing with her new mission. She needed to get focused and ready, to clear her mind, and be ready for whatever may come. Nefertara had faced little resistance in her prior missions; but you could never be too careful, or overconfident. Yes, she definitely needed to prepare herself, indeed.

*   *   *   *   *

Nyerere was at F.U.R.I.'s headquarters, wearing his uniform bottoms, praying in front of his secondary ancestral alter for his parents. He needed their wisdom and guidance, to help him to get through the issues that he's recently been struggling with. He needed to figure out what to do about Nefertara, and how he was going to heal his relationship with Amirah. He was looking for guidance and direction, having felt a bit lost, not really knowing how to handle all that was coming before him. He'd hoped that his parents would be able to point him in the right direction, and that the ancestors would help to properly guide him on how to handle these situations. His concerns were growing, and he was starting to question his ability to handle them. He felt that, now more than ever, he needed the help and guidance of his parents, revolutionary ancestors, and the Creator to find his true path, and the answers to his questions. This was the first time that, since he'd adopted this lifestyle, that he was beginning to question his role as The Black Fist. *Am I doing the right thing...? Am I going too far? Am I NOT going far enough? Should I be changing my tactics?* It was all so overwhelming for him, especially with no predecessor to properly guide him. This was uncharted territory for him, and he was practically making it up as he went along. He wanted to stop his enemies, but...did he have to slaughter all that stood in his way? He saw himself as a warrior, but even warriors have standards; a code of conduct. He'd studied many of the warrior cultures of his ancestors, not just to analyze their fighting styles, but to absorb their lifestyles; both traditional, and contemporary fighting formations such as the Umkonto WeSizwe, Deacons For Defense and Justice, and the Mau Mau. If he were to continue on this path, he needed a proper guideline to travel this path. *Where do you stand...?*, he asked himself, *What kind of a warrior do you want to be?* Will he be a merciless killer, a hired gun...? A Ronin without scruples? *What kind of a MAN do you want to be...?*

He finally opens his eyes, feeling a stirring in his soul. Nyerere finally receives his answers, and feels a weight lifting from his shoulders. His mind was now clearing, and becoming more sharply focused. He now knew what he needed to do, and he needed to do it quickly. Time was of the essence, and he needed to tackle this quickly, or all that he's ever tried to build will be all for naught. He had done too much, and had come too far, for all that he'd done to fall apart. He nods to himself, and rises. He bows to his parent's alter, saying a final prayer, and turns toward his closet. He reaches for the rest of his uniform, and gathers his weapons. *Time for some action*, he thinks to himself....

CHAPTER 16

Ray Sysm was in his own office, standing by his window. He was not in a very good mood, and was chomping down on his cigar. He was waiting for Brutality to arrive in his office, and he was adamant that he'd *better* have some good news for him. He didn't like having any type of interference affecting his business dealings, and this time was no different. There is finally a knock at his door, signaling Brutality's arrival. *It's about blasted time*, he snarls to himself. "...Come!", he barks, not bothering to turn around. Brutality enters into his office, and approaches his desk. Ray still doesn't bother to turn around to either greet, or address him, causing Brutality to feel a bit uneasy. He knew better than to get on Iggy Norance's bad side, and that went double for Ray Sysm. "My connection got whacked...", Ray gruffly replies, "...What have you gotten about it?".

"...Not much, sir. Even the police are stumped-..."
"...-I want answers, damn it! Find that damn savage, and eliminate his ass, already!"
Brutality briefly pauses. "Honestly, sir...this time...I don't think that it was him."

Ray Sysm finally turns to him, an incredulous look on his face. Brutality could see the veins popping along his neck and forehead, and knew that he had to tread very carefully, and needed to choose his words correctly the next time he opened his mouth. "What do you mean...*you DON'T think that it's him*?!?!", Ray barks. Brutality pauses, swallowing hard, trying not to piss him off.

"From past experiences...It's not his style."

"What the hell does *that* mean?!"

"Usually when he attacks any of our operations...it's his way of exposing us, and our operations..."

"Yeah...so?!?!"

"Well, with these recent setbacks...it's almost like he's targeting these contacts individually. Like...he's doesn't even *know* that we're associated with them...or just doesn't care. That's *not* how he operates." He pauses. "He's a pain in our ass...but he's a somewhat *predictable* pain in the ass."

Ray pauses, letting what was said sink in. He starts to reflect on the attacks to their other operations that they'd recently suffered. From what he knew about their encounters against The Black Fist, what Brutality was saying actually made sense. It started to make him more frustrated, the more he thought about it. "Well, then...", he blusters, "If not him...then *who*?".

"That...I *don't* know."

"What do you *mean*...you *don't* know?!?!"

"Whoever this guy is...he's different. There's no method to his madness...so to speak."

"Great...", Ray snarls to himself, "Just what we need...*another* wild animal to deal with!" He momentarily fumes. "...Damn it! This is infuriating!"

"...We're on it. I'm putting some of my best operatives on it, as well as the Commissioner. We're *going* to nail his ass, and make him pay for all that he's done to us, and our operations!"

"...-See that you do! The *last* thing that we need is to embolden these savages!"

"We *won't* let that happen! He's as good as caught."

"...-See that he is!", Ray snaps.

Brutality nods to him, turns, and exits out of his office. He closes the door behind him, and lets out a huge breath. He *never* wanted to have an encounter with Ray Sysm like that again. They'd easily replaced Ovie by hiring him in his place; they wouldn't hesitate to do the same to *him* if he failed at his job. Of course, he didn't have the same restrictions holding him back as when he was on the police force. Brutality smiles to himself; he knew that he could gather his people to storm the streets, and start cracking a few heads to find out who's been messing with their operations. *Maybe this won't be so bad*, he thinks to himself, *Whoever you are...your days are NUMBERED!* He heads towards his own office, pulls out his phone, and starts contacting his operatives, barking orders, and making plans.

CHAPTER 17

Sekhmet Baset has made her way over to the edge of the Warehouse District, close to the docks. The information that she'd gotten from the antiquities smuggler lead her here, to where he occasionally stored some of his ill gotten wears. This particular warehouse was known as a smuggler's paradise, where a lot of illegal wares got stored; narcotics, weapons, antiquities, stolen goods, etc. They hadn't started gentrifying this part of the city yet, so it was easy to hide their hot goods out here; out of sight, and out of mind. It was a haven for a lot of dealers and smugglers, and they took advantage of its locale, and the lack of security in this sector of the city. It was nowhere near as bad as it was in years past, but it was still a stronghold for illicit activities, nonetheless.

Sekhmet Baset had easily dispatched with the men stationed at the loading dock. They were clumsy brutes with no real fighting skills; just meatheads who thought that they could rush her. *Fools...*, she thought to herself, *useless brutes, who believe that they can be warriors. Pathetic!* She makes her way further inside, dispatching a few of the security guards working there, cutting them down with her Khopesh sword. She would let none stand in the way of her completing her mission. Penetrating her way deeper inside the warehouse, securing floor by floor, taking out all that challenged her. Sekhmet Baset finally makes her way to the upper floors, finally finding her target.

Finally..., she smiles to herself, looking at the storage unit. She easily discards with the locks, and opens the gate door. She sees the stolen antiquities still left over from the smuggler's stash; he still had other buyers for his goods, after his stopover here in New Washington City. There were many statues, busts, masks, and other cultural objects stored in there; no doubt pilfered during times of war, occupation, or even neocolonialists or rebels looking to make a quick buck for guns. She begins to gather the objects, putting them in a bag that she'd brought with her. She diligently gathers the items stored there, working quickly and swiftly.

"...-Ahem!"

Surprised, Sekhmet Baset turns around, caught completely off guard. She sees The Black Fist standing there, his arms folded across his chest, wearing a grim look on his face. "I knew it...!".

"<...-What is the meaning of this?! What are you doing here?!>"
"...-Trying to stop you."
"<*Why*?! You do *not* need to be here!>"
"...Apparently, I *do* need to be here!"
"<This is none of your business!>"
"...So, what...now you're a thief?!"

"<...-How *dare* you! I am liberating these items back to their rightful owners! They were stolen from our people...appropriating our culture for their own monetary gain!>"

"...-And those guards had to pay for it with their lives?!"

"<...-They're just as complicit!>"

"You've crossed a line, Sekhmet!"

"<...What?!>"

"...-Those guards were *innocent*! They probably didn't even know *what* was being stored in half of these units! They were just hard working men that were struggling to earn a paycheck!"

Sekhmet Baset pauses, surprised by his words. She then straightens up, and he could feel her eyes burning into him, brimming with disapproval. "<I thought that you were like me..>", she seethes, "<...I thought that you understood-...>".

"...-I *do* understand! I'm a warrior...I fight to *protect* my people!"

"<...-So do I!>"

"I'm not above eliminating any internal threats...but I *don't* wantonly kill people! *Only* in self defense....not unless they deserve it!"

Sekhmet Baset pauses. "<You're too weak! No wonder your enemies don't fear you!>"

"...-I don't *need* them to fear me! *That's* the difference!"

"<I thought that you were a true kindred spirit...one who I could truly bond with...>"

"...-You were wrong. I guess we were *both* wrong..."

"<I cannot...*will not*...change who and what I am!>"

"I am a warrior...I protect the people of this city, and beyond...", he says, unhooking his billy clubs, and twirls them in a combative manner, "...And I *will* stop you, if I have to!"

Sekhmet Baset's body shifts, he could tell that his last statement stung her. He could also tell that anger was coursing throughout her body. She unsheaths her Khopesh sword, and gets into a Kutakuta fighting stance. "<If you choose me as an enemy, as opposed to a comrade...then, come meet your fate!>", she hisses. The Black Fist gets into his own Kalinda fighting stance, ready to engage her in combat. "I'm not afraid of you, Cat...", he growls, "...And I *won't* hold back!". "<...Neither will I!>", she hisses. They begin to circle each other, looking for their opening to attack.

She sees her opening, and springs forward with her attack. They engage in heated combat, clashing their weapons against each other, trying to batter the other into submission. They throw their full skills into this fight, no longer inhibited by unfamiliarity, or even friendship; this was *war*. They viciously battle each other, throwing their full might and skill level into the contest. Sekhmet Baset slashes at him with her sword, switching styles, trying to confuse him. The Black Fist just counters her moves, also switching styles himself to keep her off balance. That fear and dread from their first encounter no longer existed; he was fighting with a renewed sense of purpose.

This was *his* city, and he was going to protect it with all of his might, will, and skills. As much as he cared for her, he couldn't let her continue with her reign of terror. She wasn't just eliminating threats...she was also killing innocents. That wasn't the type of warrior that he was, nor was that how he intended to protect the city and community. Sekhmet Baset angrily lashes out at him, feeling hurt and betrayed. She had considered him a kindred spirit, having shared a similar history, having both lost so much at a young age. They had both chosen the path of fighting behind a mask, to take down those that would harm their community, harm their people. Unfortunately, they'd chosen different strategies to achieve their shared goals.

Sekhmet Baset sees an opening, and hits The Black Fist with a shot to his ribs. He slightly buckles, backpedaling. She takes this time to mount her escape, grabbing her bag, and making a mad dash out of the room. As angry as she was with him, she still needed to complete her mission of liberating those antiquities. The Black Fist quickly recovers, and chases after her. They zig zag through the halls of the warehouse, and make their way up the staircase. They skip steps, running up the stairs, and make their way up to the roof. The Black Fist tries to cut her off, flinging a volley of throwing darts at her. Sekhmet Baset dives out of the way, rolling on the floor, and comes back up onto her feet. He throws a secondary volley, this time at her hand, causing her to drop her bag. Sekhmet Baset momentarily pauses, distracted by the loss of her bag. The Black Fist engages her again, using Kipura, pressing his attack. Sekhmet Baset counters, using

Hikuta, fending him off. They continue to heatedly clash with each other, vying to come out on top. The Black Fist throws his all against her, with Sekhmet Baset being the toughest opponent that he's ever faced. The scary part was...he still didn't know if she was friend, or foe. With her fighting skills, she was a deadly ally to have...and a scary foe to have to fight against. He continues to switch styles on her, trying to keep her off balance. She switches fighting styles herself, trying to counter him, finding him a much more difficult opponent this time around. This was no longer an enjoyable battle with a worthy opponent; this was now life, or death. She was looking to complete her mission, and he was determined to stop her, and make her pay for the deaths of those innocents that she'd caused.

The Black Fist sees an opening, and throws a foot sweep, knocking her off balance. Sekhmet Baset stumbles a bit, but quickly recovers. He presses his attack, changing tactics, and switching to styles that she seemed unfamiliar with. Sekhmet Baset seemed to be getting frustrated with this new tactic, not being able to counter the styles that he was using. The Black Fist begins to gain the upper hand in their fight, being able to knock her about. They were both breathing heavy, having expended a lot of energy during their battle. The Black Fist knocks Sekhmet Baset down with a kick, and she stumbles about, trying to regain her balance. They both pause, breathing heavy and exhausted. He shoots her a stern look. "Look...", he pants, "...Just give up already! I *don't* want to hurt you...".

"<...-Never!>"

"...This is *stupid*! I'm *not* going to kill you..."

"<...-Then, you are a *coward*!>"

"...No. I'm just not a killer."

"<I thought that we believed in the same thing...>"

"...-Don't give me that! I will *always* protect my people, and my community!"

She pauses. "<We could have truly had something together...>"

"I will *always* protect my people! I *don't* have to conquer the night to do that..."

"<Our people's enemies have to be eliminated!>"

"...-And they will be! You just have to look at the bigger picture..."

"<What do you mean?!>"

"Going after these individuals...? They're small fries...it's a waste of time and energy.

There's *always* an unseen hand guiding the madness..."

"<...-All the more reason to destroy our enemies!>"

"You're too busy channeling Sekhmet, than you are Baset!"

"<What's *that* supposed to mean?!>"

"This is a *war*! You can't win it by yourself...*won't* be able to win it by yourself." He

briefly pauses, catching his breath. "You need strategy...allies...comrades..."

"<Are you talking about me, or *yourself*?!>"

"...-I had to learn all of this the *hard* way! *You* don't have to!"

"<...What?!>"

The Black Fist pauses. He then approaches her, lowering his sports goggles, a disarming gesture on his part. Sekhmet Baset becomes surprised, letting down her guard a little bit. He crouches down near her, and lets out a weary, tired breath.

"Look...I *do* care about you. I honestly did feel like we could've had something...with, or without the masks..."

She pauses as well. "<...As did I>."

"I'm *not* gonna change my ways to the detriment of my people. I'm their protector...I accepted that responsibility the day I put on this uniform."

"<...I see.>"

"I'm *not* going to turn you in...nor, am I going to take your life. That's not who I am, or how I operate."

"<Then...how do you want to handle this...?>"

"Like I said...I could always use another revolutionary associate."

She pauses again. "...*Only* a revolutionary associate?"

"...Yes. I already have a partner."

Sekhmet Baset pauses, letting all that he's said sink in. She then slowly rises, still contemplating what was just said. "<I will think about it>", she finally replies. "That's all that I can ask", he returns, "Our struggles are all the same, both here and abroad. Our people will only be free if we link our struggles, and work *together*". She nods to him,

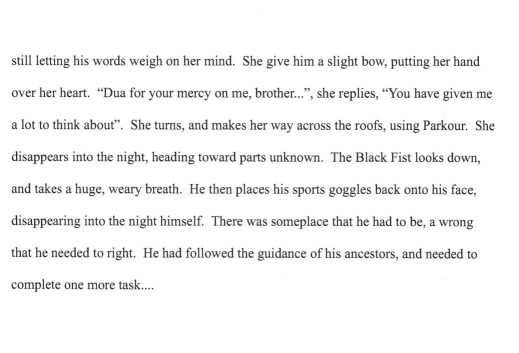

still letting his words weigh on her mind. She give him a slight bow, putting her hand over her heart. "Dua for your mercy on me, brother...", she replies, "You have given me a lot to think about". She turns, and makes her way across the roofs, using Parkour. She disappears into the night, heading toward parts unknown. The Black Fist looks down, and takes a huge, weary breath. He then places his sports goggles back onto his face, disappearing into the night himself. There was someplace that he had to be, a wrong that he needed to right. He had followed the guidance of his ancestors, and needed to complete one more task....

CHAPTER 18

Amirah was tossing and turning in her bed. She was having a hard time falling asleep, feeling tired, but restless. Though she'd had more free time in recent weeks, she was bored out of her mind. She was feeling restless, almost anxious, like she should be doing something. She lies on her back, and lets out a heavy sigh. She missed being at F.U.R.I.'s headquarters, going through their files, keeping track of Iggy Norance, The System, Brutality, and the others that were on their radar. She felt that there was a void in her life, and she missed it terribly. It also didn't make her very pleasant to be around at the station; she's had to catch herself a few time from snapping at people, and going off on suspects for no reason. Everyone could see that she was on edge, but couldn't put their finger on why. Little did they know that there was a gaping hole in her heart....

Amirah lets out another heavy sigh. She looks over at her clock, and sees the late hour of the night. She gets up, and wearily goes into her kitchen to get something to drink, and hopefully calm her nerves. She searches her near empty refrigerator, and grabs her carton of almond milk. *Yet ANOTHER thing that I have to take care of,* she bitterly thinks to herself, *Gotta go food shopping, and restock my fridge.* She closes the refrigerator door, rising from her stooped position, when she senses something.

...I'm not alone here!

She immediately turns toward her living room area, and sees a silhouette sitting there, their head in their hands. She pauses, caught off guard, and lets her eyes adjust to the darkness again. After a moment, she is able to make out the figure sitting in her living room.

"...Fist?!", she loudly whispers, "Is that you...?"
"...Yeah", he sadly replies.

She lets out a relieved breath, now calming down. She really didn't know how to feel about him being in her apartment, unannounced, but then again, it's not like he'd ever told her whenever he was coming over. She'd just gotten used to him showing up, out of the blue, especially when they were working on a case together. "Thank goodness! You scared the hell out of me...", she says. She pauses, picking up on his silence, and body language. "What are you doing here?", she asks, "What's wrong...?".

"...I'm a fuck up."
"Come, again...?"
"...I'm sorry. I shouldn't have treated you the way that I did."
"What?!"

"Coming at you, the way that I did...? It was stupid. You've always had my back, and I didn't have yours. I'm sorry..."

Could it be...?, she thinks to herself.

"Sometimes-...I don't know what I'm doing, half the time..."

"Look...there's no manual for this. We're kinda making it up as we go along..."

"I thought that this would be the best way for me to honor my parents. To keep their memories alive..." He pauses. "I can't even do *that* right..."

"You have...in your own way. You help keep the streets safe...protect the people from predators from outside, and from within..."

"...-Not without you."

Amirah sucks in her breath. She tries to control her feelings, but seems to not be able to contain them. *Is he finally going to admit it...?*, she thinks to herself, *does he feel the same as I do...?* She finally joins him, sitting in front of him on the edge of her coffee table. He finally removes his hands from his head, letting his hair hang down, his sports goggles hanging around his neck, with a look of deep sadness on his face. She takes a calming breath, pausing before she speaks. "We've been able to do a lot together...", she says.

"...-I'm not just talking about F.U.R.I."

"What?!"

"We've gotten...close...these last few years..."

"Well...yeah..."

"We've done a lot together...and maybe I haven't appreciated that enough..."

"Whoa...hold up", she says, trying not to get her hopes up, "What are you saying...?"

"Look...I have to admit, I got...excited...meeting Sekhmet Baset. I thought that I'd met a kindred spirit...someone who could really and truly identify with me..."

"I don't follow..."

"She's a legacy, just like me.... A child of the movement...the child of a movement leader..."

"...Huh?!"

"...Nefertara is Sekhmet Baset."

"...*What*?!", Amirah says, almost out loud.

"...Yet *another* thing that I should have told you. That was the thing that I needed to figure out that night..."

"Whoa...", was all Amirah could get out, shocked.

"I thought that she was like me...could *identify* with me..." He briefly pauses, becoming saddened again. "...I was wrong."

"What...what happened?"

"...Ideological differences. I can't kill for no reason. That's not the type of warrior that I am..."

"...I know", she says after a short pause, "That's what I've always respected about you."

He finally lifts his head, looking her in her eyes. "You always brought the best out of me...always had my back."

She shoots him an embarrassed smile. "You helped me to restore my faith in people, and the movement. I became a believer."

"...You did the same for me...your dedication to Jabari's case when he died...wanting to find his killer, and bring his family closure..."

Amirah flashes him an embarrassed smile. "...Of course, *you* beat me to it."

"...But, still...you cared."

"I didn't want to have another family suffer from a loss, with no answers. Too many of our people suffer that way..."

"That's what drew me to you...your spirit."

She pauses, affectionately smiling at him. "Thanks."

"You're the only person who I can truly be myself with...mask, or no mask."

Amirah's heart leaped. He was finally opening up to her, and revealing his feelings for her. It was what she always wanted, what she'd hoped for. "You really mean it...?".

"...Of course."

"Thanks. That means a lot to me."

"...You deserve it. I should have been more honest with myself about how I felt...especially about you..."

Amirah stays quiet, partially shocked, partially thrilled by his words. She affectionately smiles at him, and takes his gloved hands into hers. "I know that it's been tough...and that I haven't made things easy on my end, either...".

"...You were being true to how you felt. I should have done the same."

"...Not *completely* true. I could have said something earlier..."

"...As could I." He pauses. "But...I'm saying it now..."

"So...what *are* you saying...?", Amirah asks, smiling.

"...I want us to be together. Not just as partners...not just for the movement..."

"Then...for your heart?"

"...For my heart."

Amirah continues to smile at him. She takes his face into her hands, and passionately kisses him. It felt so good to finally feel his lips on hers, feeling the heat and the warmth of his love, the softness of his lips. Nyerere kisses her back, finally feeling free, finally feeling whole. He finally felt unburdened, feeling safe in Amirah's arms. The two continue to connect with each other, finally being free and uninhibited, wanting to explore each others soul.

PART II

CHAPTER 19

Night has claimed New Washington City. The mood is somber, and the streets are actually somewhat calm. With the arrival of the 'masked avenger', the criminal element of New Washington City has learned to tread very carefully. Many a criminal enterprise has been shut down over the last few years, as well as the incarceration of, or the elimination of, a number of crime leaders. A number of black market operations have dried up, and the criminal element has been driven deep underground. No longer do street gangs and drug crews freely roam the streets; they have now moved out of the sight of this masked marauder. His actions have even inspired others to take up the mantle of community protector, cleaning up the streets of crime and criminal activity. As the guardian of New Washington City, The Black Fist cannot be expected to watch over the city alone; others needed to pick up the slack, and help in cleaning up the streets of the city. Picking up where the Uhuru Community Defense Force left off decades ago, these newer, younger activists were doing what they could to help to preserve the safety of the city. The activists weren't the *only* ones working on aiding The Black Fist in protecting the streets of the city. There were others who have *also* chosen to wear masks, as they pick up the slack...

The Hoodrat, sporting a Grey and Black outfit with a huge rat symbol airbrushed on the front and back of his Grey hoodie, is perched over a nearby building, his brown

face overlooking the streets of Turner Heights. He was on patrol with his crew; the

Concrete Jungle Zoo Crew, a former graffiti tagging crew, now looking to clean up the

streets of this still-embattled part of the city. Though limited prosperity was finally

coming to this part of the city, it was coming slowly, as the criminal element was still

stubbornly trying to hang on to this piece of territory for dear life. Though The Black

Fist had done a lot to clean up the streets in this section of the city, there was still a lot of

work to do. From his elevated position, The Hoodrat sees a shady deal going down in

the alley intersecting Turner Avenue, and Washington Boulevard. He speaks into his

bluetooth earpiece to his other teammates. "Yo...it's about to go down. Y'all in

position...?".

"...You know it!"

"...I got you, yo!"

"...No doubt, Hoodrat!"

"...Hells yeah! Lets do this!"

"A'ight...", he says, pulling up his Grey handkerchief over his brown face, "...On my

signal..."

The shady parties share some words, and shake hands. One of the shady characters

hands the other a large duffle bag that seems quite full. He zips it open, inspects the contents, smiles, and closes it back up. He then shakes hands with the other shady

character, and has his people load some other bags into their car. The parties are about

to separate, when Hoodrat gives his signal. "Yo...!", he loudly whispers, "Go...*now*!".

The members of his crew spring out from their hiding places, and engages with

the miscreants. Caught by surprise, the miscreants quickly fall to Hoodrat, and the other

members of the Concrete Jungle Zoo Crew; Alley Cat, Road Dawg, Squirrel, Project

Pigeon, and Da Stinger batter the miscreants about, using their unique fighting skills to

take them down; Alley Cat with her acrobatic, cat-like fighting style; Road Dawg with

his more aggressive, grappling style; Squirrel and Hoodrat with a more similar boxing

style; Project Pigeon with her more bird-kung fu style; and Da Stinger with his quick

hand movements, and blade based fighting style. All dressed in varying shades of Grey,

they were protecting their block, their city, from these bunch of troublemakers; they

were going to do everything in their power to stop them from ruining their home.

"...-Hey!"

"What the hell-...?!?!?"

"Yo...we got beef!"

"...Grab the stash, and break out!"

One of the criminals grabs one of the large duffle bags, and makes a break for it. He tears down the alley, making a break for freedom. Alley Cat sees this, as she takes down one of the troublemakers. "Yo...!", she yells into her earpiece, "We gots a runner...!".

"I got you...!", Hoodrat yells, tearing after him.
"...-Wait! You need back up-...!"

Hoodrat tears after him, running at a high sprint. He was quickly gaining on him, anticipating the can of whup ass that he was going to open up on him. "Get back here...!", he hollers at him. The runner then stops running and turns to him, whipping around, and pulls out a strange looking gun. Hoodrat's eyes go wide, caught completely off guard by this move, and dives out of the way at the last minute.

...Click!
"....-Oh sh-...!"
Ka-blam, ka-blam, ka-blam!!!!

Hoodrat dives and rolls out of the way, hiding behind a nearby dumpster, and crouches down for safety. The runner continues to fire his gun at him, causing the dumpster to violently shake.

"Holy sh-...!"

Ka-blam, ka-blam, ka-blam!!!!

THUMP!!! Krak, krak...SMAK!!!

The gunfire ceases, and the night becomes quiet. Hoodrat momentarily pauses, not hearing any further disturbance.

What, the-...?!?!

"Hoodie...", a gravelly voice calls out, "...You can come out, now..."

The Hoodrat pauses, then carefully peers out from behind the dumpster. He looks out, and sees The Black Fist standing over the runner who is now laying on the ground, unconscious. He had his clubs out, having apparently surprised the gunman from above, and had given him a serious beat down. The Hoodrat rises from his shelter, and makes his way over to them, strolling over to him in his urban strut, trying to cover up the fact that he was embarrassed at being saved. "I woulda had him...", Hoodrat says.

"Would've...could've...*didn't.*"

"...Showoff!"

"You were careless...and reckless."

"...He got lucky."

"...-And he almost killed you."

"...He woulda ran out of bullets. Besides...I was just about to make my move-..."

"...-Look at the dumpster."

The Hoodrat looks over at the dumpster, and becomes surprised. There were huge holes running through it, several of them inches from where he was crouched down. He tries to play it off, not wanting to show that he was shocked. "So, he was packin' some heavy hardware...", Hoodrat sarcastically says.

"...-All the more reason for you to be more careful."

"...-Awright already! Enough with the lectures!"

"Where's the rest of your crew...?"

"...Rounding up his partnahs. Had a deal going down a few blocks back..."

"...Drugs?"

"From the size of the bags they was carryin'...? It musta been somethin' bigger."

The Black Fist pauses. He didn't like when business deals were going down around the city, and he wasn't aware of it. F.U.R.I. had always provided him with intelligence in real time, letting him know about any illicit activities that were going down. He didn't like going in blind, and having some new epidemic arise under his watch. "I'll look into it...", he says to The Hoodrat. The Hoodrat just simply shrugs, and starts to walk off. "...Suit y'self, yo", he says. He starts making his way back to the rest of his crew, when

The Black Fist calls out to him.

"...-Hoodie!"

"Yeah...?", he asks, turning to him.

"...Good work."

The Hoodrat pauses, shocked at receiving praise from The Black Fist. He was actually quite excited about that, but didn't want to show himself as a fanboy. He just nonchalantly shrugs, and continues to walk off. "No doubt...", he says, "...It's all good". The Hoodrat continues on, returning back to his crew. He hides the fact that he has a big smile now plastered on his brown face, covered up by his Grey handkerchief, proud to be praised by his hero and idol. The Black Fist watches him walk off, and a worried feeling courses through his body. Something big was brewing, and was going to require all of his attention, skills, and resources. He picks up the gun that the shooter was carrying, and inspects it. *I should take this to Amirah...*, he thinks to himself; her expertise in firearms would interest her in this case. It was big and unusual looking, and was obviously quite powerful. He was starting to get a bad feeling.....

CHAPTER 20

Amirah makes her way to her most recent crime scene, this one in Banneker Heights. Apparently, there had a been a shootout in one of the local parking lots, and there were bodies strewn everywhere. She was a little annoyed to have been called out to this latest murder, getting the chance to spend an evening in with Nyerere, and *not* have to be consumed with F.U.R.I. business. At least she was in a better mood at this crime scene, and not ready to bite someone's head off, like she usually is. As she makes her way past the yellow tape, she sees Detective Abbey Lishonist stooped over one of the bodies. Abbey turns to her, and shoots her a smirk. "Hey, Amirah...", she calls out.

"...What you got, Abbey?"

"Fifteen bodies...five in a bus on their way to the hospital...three of them were D.O.A."

Amirah lets out a shocked whistle. "A drive-by...or a rumble?"

"...Honestly, we still can't tell. We're still trying to identify the players..."

"Well...this *is* Stono Boulevard. The Rebels pretty much have this place on lock..."

"...Didn't they turn over a new leaf recently, though?"

"...So they say. Actions speak louder than words."

Amirah pauses, looking around at the terrain. There were large holes in the walls of the surrounding buildings, and huge holes blown into the ground of the lot. This causes her eyebrows to furrow. "Are they doing some sort of digging, or construction around here...?", she asks, looking at the holes.

"...Nope. That's the *other* thing that's scaring the hell out of everyone out here. What witnesses we could find, they said it sounded like rumbling thunder, and loud explosions. We show up, and see this..."

"This is all from *gunfire*...?!?!", Amirah asks, completely shocked.

"...That's what the witnesses say."

Amirah pauses, shocked. She hadn't heard anything from their contacts about any type of new weapons that were supposed to be hitting the streets. They *especially* didn't need any new weapons hitting the streets of New Washington City. They were just starting to recover from their dormancy after the riots of the 90s; they didn't need a new wave of trouble hitting the streets, turning them into rivers of blood. As Amirah was lost in though, Abbey notices how Amirah's mood has changed in recent weeks, and how calm and content she now seemed. A devilish smile crosses her face. "Apparently, I must have messed up a pretty good night for you...", Abbey snickers.

"...-Huh?!?!?", Amirah returns, shocked and embarrassed.

"Come on, Amirah...", Abbey laughs.

"What...?"

"Amirah...you're glowing brighter than these spotlights we've got set up!"

An embarrassed smiles slips from her face. Amirah and Nyerere had been exploring each other, now having made their relationship official. It felt great to finally be free and uninhibited about her feelings for him, and to be able to show him how she truly feels. Their union made the more trying parts of her life more bearable to deal with, especially with issues concerning her job. "He's a good guy...a decent catch", she lets slip out.

"...Does he have a brother?"

"Sorry, no."

"Awww. Sucks to be me, then..."

"...You'll find someone, Abbey."

"Eh...I'll live. Just as long as it's none of *these* neanderthals on the force..."

Amirah lets out a short laugh, shaking her head. Abbey continues to devilishly smirk at her. The more that she'd gotten to know Abbey, the more that she liked her. She was glad that Abbey'd decided to become a sympathizer for F.U.R.I., and help out with information whenever she could. "Keep me informed, detective...", Amirah says, "...And tell John that I said hello".

"...No problem, detective."

"I'll see what I can find out on my end."

"...Will do!"

Amirah waves goodbye to her, and exits the crime scene. She was starting to grow concerned with the high body count, and the weaponry that was being used. The *last* thing that the streets needed was a new street war, with heavy and powerful artillery being used by one, if not *both* sides. She knew that she was going to have to dig deep into F.U.RI.'s contacts to see if a similar M.O. was popping up anywhere around the country, if not the rest of the diaspora. *Looks like we've got our work cut out for us*, she thinks to herself. If there was ever a time when she needed to feel safe in Nyerere's arms, it was now. An affectionate smile involuntarily starts to spread across her face. She always looked forward to spending time with him, whether at F.U.R.I's headquarters, or at either of their apartments; as long as they were together, she didn't care where. She makes her way over to her car, starts the engine, and pulls off, pulling out her secret smartphone...

CHAPTER 21

The streets of Tubman Heights were on the quiet side, tonight. Gentrification hadn't fully claimed over this area, though there were still issues affecting this section of town. Flare ups still existed between the residents, and the police force in this area; no love had been lost between the two sides, especially not with the arrival of The Black Fist. The criminal element also had to watch their backs here; no longer did they have the free reign to run the streets, like once before. It gave a sense of calm and tranquility back to the neighborhood, a feeling that had been long missing in the community for some time now. People were feeling more confident now, were more willing to come together more, and were more willing to reach out, and help each other.

A figure makes their way across the rooftops, moving at a steady pace. They jump and flip about, using Parkour, making their way across the city. The figure finally comes to a stop, and scopes out a building on Newton Avenue in west Tubman Heights. The figure peers over the ledge of the building, shielding himself from sight, avoiding the glare of the dimly lit streetlights. He sports a loose fitting, short-sleeved red hoodie, with a black cutoff shirt over it. His green baggy jeans flowed underneath him, stuffed into black boots. His red baseball cap is pulled down over his ebony face, helping to hide his features, along with his black eye mask. His eyes narrow as he scans the streets, especially the building across the street. He sees the graffiti on the side of the building, with the letters 'CJZC' written in block letters, bordered by paw prints and insect wings. His eyes continue to narrow, grunting a bit in annoyance. *Buncha clowns....*, he thinks to himself, *they think this is a game?! This ain't no game.....this serious business...!.* He then turns his head towards his left, focusing his attention on some street kids that were apparently up to no good. They were known as part of a local drug crew that was still operating in the area, and weren't being very discreet about it. It made his temper rise, as he angrily grips the ledge of the rooftop. *Buncha punks bringing down the neighborhood...*, he seethes to himself, *They're just pathetic...no better than the corrupt cops flippin' on everybody that lives here....* He raises his hood over his head, and moves in to engage them. *It's showtime...*, he thinks to himself. He makes his way across the roof, and down the fire escape of a nearby building, and lays in wait...

Two of the crew members are smoking some weed in one of the alleys, away from the others, not wanting to share their stash with the rest of their crew. The strong aroma of cannibus fills the air around them, its strong smell letting all know of its high quality. They pass the rolled blunt between each other, taking turns pulling drags from it, sometimes coughing, being overcome by the strength of the weed. They are so focused on getting high, that they don't even sense an extra presence in the alley with them....

"Pssst! Yo, son...let me get a hit of that."

"What-...?"

SMAK!!!

The taller boy catches a face full of fist, instantly falling down, immediately losing consciousness. His smoking partner is caught so off guard, yelling out, not even knowing how to react. "Yo-...!", was all he was able to get out, before catching a face full of a boot.

Pa-WAK!

He hits the ground as well, dazed and barely conscious. He looks up, and the last thing that he remembers seeing is a black shirt, and red baseball cap and hoodie staring down at him, and then a boot flying into his face...

          *   *   *   *   *

Malachi was getting himself ready to call it a day. He was putting his camera away, and shutting down his computer, when he sees Nzinga quickly striding up to him, a gleam in her eye. He was actually looking forward to going home, and catching a game, or two on the tube, or hoping to be able to just relax and unwind. He was actually enjoying having some free time, and being able to relax at home watching television, or with a lady friend that he'd recently gotten involved with. He was hoping that it was going to be one of those nights, until he sees the gleam in Nzinga's eye. He then knew that it had to be a juicy story, and was ready for anything. She had gotten him this far in his career, and was hoping to pile on a few more accolades, before calling it a career, and settling down. "Ooooh...!", he calls out, getting excited, "What have you got?".

"Heard it over the police scanner...a street crew in Tubman Heights just got taken down!"

"...What?! Who...?"

"...Newton Avenue Panthers! The cops responded to reports of gunfire, and then when they showed up....the entire crew had been taken out!"

"No way!" Malachi pauses. "You think it was our boy...?"

"...That's what *we* have to find out!"

"...I'm right behind you!", he says, grabbing his camera bag.

They gather their belongings, and rush out the door, excitedly making their way to the crime scene. They'd always enjoyed chronicling the exploits of The Black Fist, highlighting his efforts to cleanup the city. The people needed to continue to know of his efforts, and not be mislead by the powers that be that are running, or should we say *ruining*, the city. They need to help spread the positive news of their city, and continue to keep the culture alive. Yes, the Griot's Call must continue to serve the people, and be their unheard voice...

CHAPTER 22

We come to an abandoned gas station & service garage located in Southern Douglass Heights, on North Star Boulevard. The block is only partially abandoned, with a few boarded up storefronts, and business properties from bygone days. Though Douglass Heights didn't suffers as badly during the riots, it's still suffered from economic depression in the aftermath of the riots. The street is dimly lit, the city not caring, or interested, in fixing up this part of the city, though the college was only several blocks away. The residents in this area were still struggling to make due, still refusing to let go of all that they had, what they have been able to maintain, despite the lack of capital. The strongest remnants of the movement still maintained out here, and were going to preserve this part of the city, if it was the last thing they were going to do.

He makes his way inside, his hoodie covering his head, making his way through the unlocked hatch on the roof. He shimmies his way inside through the crawlspace, and finally makes it inside the gas station. He lets out a deep and weary sigh, and makes his way towards the back into the service garage, fingering his face. One of the members of the drug crew caught him with a shot to his face, and he needed to take care of his injuries. *Got sloppy out there*, he chides himself, *I can't get sloppy like that out in the field. That'll get me killed....* He looks in the makeshift mirror that he has, and fingers his bruise, getting some ointment to treat it. *HE'D never get sloppy like that*, he chides himself again, *I've gotta do better.* He takes off the baseball cap and face mask, exposing his very young, ebony face, his hair done in cornrows; no older than his late teens, to very early twenties. He wearily sighs at his reflection, finally putting the ointment on his bruise. He slightly winces at the pain, slightly hissing at the sting of it. He finishes putting the ointment on his bruises, and looks in the mirror, heavily sighing again. He'd seen the hell that the neighborhood had gone through over the years, and wanted so badly to be a part of that change. The drugs, the crime, the brutality of the local police...it not only infuriated him, but also made him feel quite powerless. It wasn't until the arrival of The Black Fist, that he'd felt any hope at all. If *HE* could make a difference in the community, then, why couldn't he do the same thing, himself?

He lets out another weary breath, and walks away from the mirror, rotating his sore arm. He pulls off his black sleeveless shirt and red hoodie, exposing his muscle-toned chest, and makes his way over to his makeshift workout area. He had makeshift workout equipment that he had scavenged from some of the remaining equipment from the garage; car tires as free weights, a rolled up mattress as a punching bag, a bench press, a chin up bar. He was serious about his mission, unlike those clowns from the other side of town, the Concrete Jungle Zoo Crew. He was going to make sure that the streets were going to be cleaned up, just Like the Black Fist would do. He didn't want any child to suffer like he did growing up, with these lawless, crime infested streets, and the pervasiveness of drugs. No...no other young person was going to have to suffer like that, not if *HE* had anything to say about it. He makes his way over to his makeshift punching bag, and starts to pound away at it, focusing his determined passions toward it. He needed to get better at combat, if he were to clean up the streets. No more sloppy attacks...time to get down to business. *I need to get better...*, he thinks to himself, as he pounds away at the bag. His posters of revolutionary heroes surrounded the workout area, encouraging him on with his mission and drive. He continues to whack away at his punching bag, channeling the energies of his revolutionary heroes and ancestors. He needed to get better....*be* better. Much better...

CHAPTER 23

The sun has set, and the starry night sky covers New Washington City. As the city ends yet another busy day, the creatures of the night come out to play, and start to make their rounds. Brutality was highly nervous, though he didn't want it to show. They we having a private dinner at one of the fancier restaurants in the heart of Metro New Washington, closed to the public. Many of the heavy hitters were here in attendance, and he was quite flabbergasted to be among them. Iggy Norance and Ray Sysm, as well as Ray's brother Sexton "Sex" Sysm, along with the Governor Wyatt Supremacy, as well as his old friend, and new State A.G., Wyatt Privilege. Also seated at the dinner table were some of the older guard that had run the city during its heyday; former-Police Commissioner Jim Crow, and former-D.A. William "Willie" Lynch, as well as the old former-City Council President Deon "Dee" Scrimination, who now works in the private sector, having on occasion worked with Ray and Iggy in recent years. It was awe-inspiring to be surrounded by so many men of power, in one room. It was fine dining on lavish china, away from prying eyes, with glasses filled with the finest of wines and bourbon. Their cigar smoke filled the air of the room, creating a mysterious fog-like mist throughout the room. It made Brutality feel good to be a part of this, and to be surrounded by men of such prestige and power. "Well, gentlemen...", Privilege boasts, "Looks like another victory toast is in order. Looks like our boy is going to have another landslide victory...".

"He better...", Ray snorts, "...After what we've invested in him, we *better* get a return on our investment!"

"Please...", Iggy guffaws, "...*Nothing* happens in this city unless we *let* it happen."

"He keeps the savages in line...", Supremacy states, "...And *we* get to have our way. It's a win-win situation."

"...Perhaps", Ray concedes.

"He's useful. That's why Wyatt and I picked him", Iggy states matter-of-factly.

Privilege condescendingly smiles. "...He plays the role, and the animals blindly follow him. It's all for our benefit...as it *should* be."

"Quite calculating, and meticulous...", Dee chuckles, "...Not like back in *our* day, eh Willie, Jim?"

"The savages knew their place, back then...", Jim says, "...You put down a few of those animals, and they would back down."

"...Unfortunately, some of them started to get bold", Willie grunts, "...And became a major pain in our asses, afterward..."

"Apparently, some things still haven't changed", Sex interjects, "These animals are *still* causing us some problems..."

"...-It's nothing", Brutality interjects, "...They'll be dealt with, soon enough."

"Easy, Joseph...easy", Supremacy soothes, "No one is pointing any fingers here...just airing out our grievances. No one is questioning your efforts..."

It made Brutality feel good that he had the support of such men with stature. He nods

his head, conceding his point, and continues to enjoy the meal. "No problems here,

Joe...not from *me*", Jim comments, "You did a *fine* job after I stepped down". "Thank

you, Commissioner...", Brutality compliments, "...That means a lot coming from you".

"Your *replacement*, however...", he continues, "Seems to be dropping the ball a bit..."
"...Why do you think I got rid of him?", Iggy guffaws.
"He *still* hasn't found, or killed that blasted savage", Ray bristles.
"*Again*...why do you think I got rid of him?", Iggy reiterates, "...I *don't* tolerate

incompetence."
"He's allowed that blasted savage to become a jungle king", Dee nastily comments,

shaking his head, "...He's emboldening the other savages to rebel, and stand up against

us."
"...It won't last...", Willie derisively says, "...They're a spineless lot."
"...All the more reason for us to double down on our commitment to keep them from

achieving any sort of real power", Privilege states.
"...Here, here!", Supremacy states, raising his glass.

The other men nod in agreement, and also raise their glasses. *They* were the powers that made society function, and they would be damned if they were going to let anybody challenge their right to power; *especially* those that they considered to be inferior to them. "To the powers that be, gentlemen...", Supremacy says, toasting the others in the room.

"...To the powers that be!"

They tip their glass to each other, and down their drink of choice. They continue on with their meal, enjoying each others company, and making plans for the future.

*   *   *   *   *

As night has fallen over the city, A. Simi was wrapping up some business at his campaign headquarters in Dubois Hills, from earlier in the day. Though he personally liked Ovie Seere, he was growing concerned with some of the recent rashes of gun violence that had been happening all over the city. It wasn't good for his image, and almost hurt him in the polls. His victory was still assured, but he never wanted to hedge his bets. He needed to shore up his support base, and make sure that *nothing* was going to impede his chances of being re-elected. It made him weary to be so concerned with the campaigning side of politics; he just wanted to do his job, and help to improve the city. He'd help to usher in a new wave of economic prosperity into the city, and create a new renaissance. Things were improving, and he had even bigger plans for the city during his second term. The meeting with Ovie, Gait Keeper, Orr Reo, and City Council President Petite Bourgeoisie-Boulé had gone over pretty well, even though things did get a little testy between Petite, and Ovie; she had chided him on his ineffectiveness with the recent murders, and the rash of shootings that have been happening in the city, and he took exception to that. At the same time, just because he liked him personally, didn't meant that he wouldn't replace him, if need be. He needed to secure his place as mayor, and any dead weight that jeopardized that, would have to be replaced.

Ovie finally leaves, not in the best of moods. Orr Reo, and Gait also decide to call it a night as well, and also exit his office. Petite watches them leave, and then turns to A. Simi. "That meeting actually went pretty well...", she comments.

"...Except for Ovie. I don't think he took too kindly to your criticizing his policing tactics."

"He's a big boy...", she derisively snorts, "...He can handle it."

"Still...he's good people."

"Yeah...anyway...", she replies, rolling her eyes, "Sometimes they need a fire lit under them, once in a while. *We're* the ones running things, now. They need to be reminded of that..."

"...True."

"Looks like it's going to be another landslide election..."

"It wouldn't hurt...just as long as I win."

"...You will", she slightly purrs, "I can be *very* convincing when need be."

"...That's true", he laughs.

They give each other a smile, and Petite seductively crosses her legs in front of him. For an older woman, she kept herself in *very* good shape, showing off her shapely golden form. Though they did spar with each other from time to time during his administration, there were also many moments of fun and games, between them. Her eyes were now speaking coded messages to him, and he knowingly smiles. She was powerful and savvy, but was also quite alluring. That made her a dangerous enemy to have, but also a powerful ally to look out for...and an intriguing woman to get to know, personally. Her marriage was primarily for status and wealth, and the acquisition of political power during her coming up; there were rumors and stories of her infidelity with other members of the city council, and other men of notoriety...nothing that was ever substantiated, though. Were those stories from jealous political rivals, hoping to bring her down, or was she *really* that devious? A. Simi knew better, as she had been able to school him during his administration, not just politically. Petite finally gets up from her chair, and saunters her way over to him, finally sitting at the edge of his desk, hiking up her skirt just a bit, continuing to expose her shapely, toned legs. The intense smell of her sweet perfume resonated in his nostrils, enticing him. The look in her light brown eyes spoke tongues to him, and he could feel the heat emanating from her body. "You look stressed from all of this election talk...", she purrs at him, "...You look like you need a comforting massage".

"Really, now?"

"...Yes."

"I should make an appointment, then."

"Oh...you don't have to do all that, Mr. Mayor...", she coos, "...*I* can help you to relax."

"...Is that right?"

"...But, of course. It's the least that I can do for you, after all of the help that you've given me during your administration."

"...as long as it's nothing inappropriate."

"...I wouldn't dream of it."

"Just as long as the wall don't talk."

"...*I'll* never tell."

A. Simi returns a devilish smile to her, and Petite leans in, giving him a seductive kiss. They continue to feats on each others lips, as A. Simi slides his chair back, allowing it to recline, making room for two...

CHAPTER 24

Hoodrat and Project Pigeon were on patrol, keeping their eyes on the streets, looking out for any trouble that may come their way. It had been a slow night in Turner Heights, and so they'd decided to expand their patrol into neighboring Banneker Heights. Since the entire crew was out on patrol, they didn't feel that they all needed to be patrolling in the same area. As it is, Hoodrat actually *enjoyed* spending time with Project Pigeon; she wasn't as obnoxious as some of his other team members, not having an oversized ego, or anything. She was actually rather on the quiet side, which is what also made her such a deadly opponent; she let her fists do all of her talking for her. Her long, dark Grey faded poncho cloaked her physical features, covering up the fact that she was actually quite diminutive. But, when she was flying at you with her fighting skills, she really did look somewhat like a bird of prey. It was why Hoodrat liked her, and asked her to join his crew, not just as a bad ass graf artist, but also when he decided to fight crime, and protect the streets, being influenced by The Black Fist. The hood of her faded poncho cloaked her Blasian features, hiding her brown face, and oblique almond eyes that pierced into your soul. Her stoic silence made many others uncomfortable, but intrigued Hoodrat. She was *definitely* the perfect person to become a member of his crew...

Tonight's patrol was growing quite boring; many of the miscreants seeming to have been able to find hiding spaces, staying out of sight. The dimly lit streets from their elevated position showed no signs of activity, not even so much as a stray shopping bag flying in the breeze. It made Hoodrat's attention wander, now scoping out some of the nearby buildings, checking them out as a potential canvas for his latest throw-up. He had been working on an idea for a new piece, and was itching to tag up a wall somewhere. "Man...this be *borin'*, sometimes!", he complains. Pigeon's eyes shift towards his direction, but says nothing. She lets out a bit of a sigh, basically agreeing with him. "I need some action...", he states, "...Or, a least a wall to tag up. Man, just...*somethin'*!". Pigeon suddenly shifts her head to her left, her eyes narrowing, her energy completely changing. Hoodrat picks up on this, and looks at her, now concerned. "What...?", he asks.

"...Over there!", she says, pointing.

Hoodrat turns to the direction where she's pointing. A few blocks away, he sees someone running across the rooftops, moving at a high clip. He sees the figure wearing the revolutionary colors, but could tell even from that far away, that the figure had more of a street sensibility to them. Hoodrat's eyes now narrow, pulling up his handkerchief to cover up his face. "Let's go...", he says, "...Somethin' don't smell right 'bout this...". Pigeon nods, and they take off after the figure, jumping across the rooftops.

He uses Parkour to make his way across the rooftops, seeking out any miscreants that were out and about, wanting and waiting to dispense justice out on the streets. Word on the street was that some dirty cops were supplying some gangbangers with some hardware, feeding into the gang violence that was still plaguing this part of the city. He aimed to put an end to that, and finally rid the streets of both the criminal element, and the corrupt cops...for *good*. No one man should be responsible for cleaning up the streets by himself, and he was going to make sure that he was going to do his part. He finally makes his way over to a tenement building on Southeast Avenue, and peers into an alleyway. His eyes narrow, as he sees the Crown Victoria of two plainclothes officers, patiently sitting in their car. He could see them laughing and joking with each other, snidely smiling. His anger grows, becoming infuriated with their callousness. *They destroy this community, and then LAUGH about it*, he seethes to himself, *Oh yeah...they're gonna PAY for this...!*. He bristles even more, as a small group of bangers rolls up on the cops, looking to do business. He prepares himself, ready to make his move...

"...-Yo...!", a voice calls out to him, "...Who, you?!"

He whirls around, completely caught off guard, not expecting anyone to be on the roof with him. He sees Hoodrat and Project Pigeon intently staring at him, their body posture screaming '*confrontation*' at him. He grows angry, and loudly whispers at them through gritted teeth, "...Get the hell outta here!".

"Yo...what the hell-..?!"

Yo...it's a set up!"

...-Break out!"

Pap, pap, pap, pap, pap, pap!!!

Gunfire then erupts, with bullets whizzing by his ears, causing him to cry out, and duck

behind the ledge. The sound of car tires squealing and taking off floods his ears, causing

his agitation to increase. *Damn it...*, he angrily seethes,...*they're gonna get away!*.

Hoodrat and Project Pigeon split away from each other, jumping into action. They make

their way down to the streets from opposite sides of the building, flying down the fire

escape, hoping to cut off the routes of escape for the shooters. Hoodrat is able to make it

down first, and is able to sucker punch one of the gang members shooting at them,

catching him as he tries to flee the alley, causing him to instantly hit the ground.

Hoodrat stands over him, ready to finish him off, when bullets strike the wall that he's

standing next to.

Ka-pap, ka-pap, ka-pap, ka-pap, ka-pap!!!

"...-Oh, f-...!!!"

He dives out of the way, using the wall as protection. He takes a few moments to calm down, and then grows annoyed. "What *is* it wit mu'fuckas shooting at me, lately?!", he yells, more to himself. He then hears the sounds of screams of pain, and the pounding of flesh.

Pap..smak...whop...KRAK!!

He peeks out from behind the wall, and sees Project Pigeon engaging the remaining gang members in hand-to-hand combat, having disarmed them. He races down the alley, and joins her, battering down the gang members. He brutally pounds one of them into submission, letting his anger out on him. "...-That's for shootin' at my ass!", he spits out, punching him one final time.

They both finally pause, looking at their battered opponents lying on the floor, moaning in defeat and pain. Hoodrat turns to Pigeon, concerned for his teammate. "You good..?", he asks her. He just sees her looking upward towards the roof of the building, never averting her steely gaze from skyward. He looks up in the same direction as she, and sees the mystery stranger angrily staring down back at them. He then turns, and quickly exits. "Hey...!", Hoodrat calls out, "...Come back here!". He races towards the fire escape that he used to make his way down to the streets, and races back towards the roof. By the time he and Pigeon finally make it back up there, the

Mystery Man is now gone, doing Parkour across the rooftops, moving at a fast clip.

Hoodrat watches him as he moves, bewildered. *Who the hell was THAT?!*, he asks

himself. He then reaches for his phone...

CHAPTER 25

Amirah and Nyerere are spending time at F.U.R.I.'s headquarters, actually taking some time to relax. Amirah had finally taken some approved vacation time, and was spending it helping to update and retool some of F.U.R.I.'s functions, and add some contacts to the network. Nyerere was also trying to convince her to actually *relax* during her vacation, and was trying to instruct her in some Kemetic yoga techniques that he'd learned. Unfortunately, they'd let their carnal desire for each other get in the way, and ended up having an intense lovemaking session, instead. They were lying in his makeshift bed, resting up and enjoying each others company, readying themselves for another round of intense lovemaking. The buzzing of one of their secret smartphones goes off, causing them both to groan at the interruption. Now that they were together as a couple, they wanted to explore their relationship, and each other, as often as possible. There passion fueled each other, and brought them closer together, making this mission a personal one for them to rid the world of the Powers That Be that oppressed their people, empowering them to continue the fight. Amirah lets it ring a few more times, and then finally answers it, not in the best of moods. "The all-seeing Third Eye...", she flatly says into the phone.

"Yeah...ummmm...", Hoodrat starts, sounding somewhat unsure.

"What's wrong, Hoodie?"

"Yeah, ummm....where's our boy at?"

Amirah becomes confused, not knowing what he was getting at, turning to Nyerere, now sporting a concerned look. "He's here at HQ...", she replies, somewhat confused, and a little annoyed, "Why...?".

"Soooo...he's *not* out here in Banneker Heights, runnin' across the rooftops..?"

"...*What*?!", she says, now sitting up.

"...Rockin' a new outfit, I might add..."

Amirah pauses, her mind now running, full of deep concern. She then throws off the covers, and heads straight for the computer station, putting the phone on speakerphone, totally oblivious to her nude state. She puts the phone on a holder, and mercilessly taps away at the keys of the computer. "Hoodie...give me your location", she commands.

"...-Forget that...he's gettin' away! Headin' north of the city. Looks like he's headin' towards Downtown New Washington City...."

"Can you follow him?"

"He's got a good head start on us. Ran into some bangaz makin' a deal for gats, with some plainclothes lookin' to make a quick buck..."

"...Do what you can. I'm calling in some back up..."

"Got'chu! Hoodrat out!"

Amirah continues to mercilessly tap away at the computer console, punching up a map of the city, trying to anticipate and triangulate the trajectory of the Mystery Man's escape. Nyerere saunters over to her, a devilish smile on his face. He hands her one of his spare vests, thoroughly amused. "Thought that you might want to put this on...", he chuckles, "...It can get kinda cold in here". Amirah pauses, turning to him, slightly confused. She then looks down at her naked state, and starts to blush. "Um...I got a little caught up in the moment...", she says, now wearing an embarrassed smile, slipping on the vest.

"Hey...you won't hear *me* complaining about it! I *liked* what I was seeing."
"...Nasty ass."
"Hey...conscious brothers have a freaky side, too, ya know..."
"Okay...", she laughs, "...You got that one..."
"...Only for my queen, though."
"Thank you." She pauses, affectionately looking at him. "Be safe...and hurry back?"
"...Will do."

They give each other a quick and passionate kiss, and then concentrate on their duties. Nyerere whisks off, changing into his uniform, as Amirah concentrates on triangulating this Mystery Man's location, and contacting backup for Hoodrat and The Black Fist.

*   *   *   *   *

He makes his way back to Douglass Heights, not in the best of moods. Those damn rookies from CJZC messed up his operation, and probably allowed those cops and gang bangers to escape. He was primarily upset with himself, moreso at the fact that he'd allowed himself to be snuck up upon. What if they had been gang bangers on patrol...? He'd be captured, if not *dead*, by now. He really needed to improve his skills, if he were to continue to do this. Sloppiness, and faulty instincts could *not* be tolerated. That could get someone killed, mainly himself. At least he had the satisfaction of losing those damn rookies along the rooftops, having lost them after they'd caught up to him by the Warehouse District. As much as those rookies annoyed him, he had to give them their respect; they were pretty good at trailing him. They had dogged determination, and were going to follow him to no end. If he hadn't given them the slip through a few of those abandoned warehouses, they might have actually found his secret hideout. He finally makes his way back towards the gas station & service garage. He looks around one last time, making sure that he wasn't followed, and makes his way over to the overhead entrance. He makes his way inside the gas station, and walks towards the back area, where the service garage is. He heavily and wearily sighs, hanging his head a bit, feeling saddened at the failure of this most recent mission. He was hoping to have made a difference tonight, but ended up screwing up, letting those two rookies sneak up on him. It made him start to really question his skills...

As he is about to pulls off his face mask and hat, his senses start to scream for his attention, the hairs on the back of his neck now perking up, a feeling of dread now filling his soul.

...Danger!

He looks up, and throws a back fist, sensing that someone was behind him. He strikes nothing but air, but feels a sharp pain from below, as he is hit in the jaw by a blow so fast and hard, that he didn't even see it coming.

...-KRAK!!!

He is lifted up off the ground by the hard blow, and flies backwards in the air, slightly losing consciousness. He is brought back to reality when he crashes hard onto a makeshift table that he'd set up, breaking it. Pain sears through his body, and anger floods his soul. Nobody knew of his secret hideout, and no one was even supposed to be there. Whoever this intruder was, they were about to catch a world of hurt. *Step onto MY turf...?!?!*, he angrily seethes, *yo ass is mine, punk!*. He rolls over onto his side, struggling to rise from the blow, and looks out into the darkness. He then sees someone dressed in black and white in an Kemetic motif, wearing a black cat-headed helmet mask. He steels himself, ready for combat, preparing to engage this intruder. "...-Get outta my place!", he angrily spits.

"<Stand down...>", Sekhmet Baset commands, "<...Or, I *put* you down!>"

"I don't know what you're saying...but I *don't* like your tone!"

"<Stand....down!>"

"...Last chance. Bounce!"

"<You fool...>", she replies, shaking her head.

He charges at her, full of rage, throwing several punches at her. Sekhmet easily blocks his attacks, and strikes him with sharp, precise blows to his body, causing him to backpedal in pain, having the wind knocked out of him. He looks at her, shocked by her fighting skills, and sees her getting into a Hikuta fighting stance. He then grows angry, and gets into a fighting stance of his own. *I ain't going out like this...*, he seethes, *not in MY house!*. He angrily goes after he with another barrage of punches, seeking to batter her down, and she easily blocks his blows, and hits him with a sharp shot to his ribs, dropping him down to his knees, and finally fells him with a shot to the face. He begins to lose consciousness, the world now growing dark all around him....

CHAPTER 26

...Darkness...

Muffled sounds....

Are those...voices....?

...ANGRY voices, at that....

His vision is blurred, and the world is still dark. The voices are different, male and female. And yes...one of them sounds slightly angry. "...-Part of recon and surveillance *don't* you understand?!", a gravelly male voice responds, full of annoyance.

"I told him to stand down...", a synthesized female voice curtly responds, "...He didn't!"

"..-You weren't even supposed to *be* in there!"

"...-He was an unknown enemy! I used the necessary amount of force!"

"...-He's *not* an enemy! We don't know *what* he is! That's what *recon* is for!"

"...This isn't helping...", another female voice interjects.

"...He was a threat that was neutralized! I stand by my actions!"

"...-Again...we don't know *what* he is! That's my *point!*"

The angry voices were starting to give him a headache, which was adding to the pain that he was already feeling. Worse still, was this putrid smell that was now filling his nostrils; apparently, he had something on his face that stunk. He lets out a groan, now starting to come to, the angry voices bringing him back to reality. "Nggggghhhhhh...", he lets out, having trouble focusing his eyes.

"...He's coming to", Hoodrat lets out.

He tries to sit up, pain shooting from his face and his ribs. He can tell that he has a wet cloth covering his eyes, which was probably why he couldn't see very clearly. He struggles to sit up, taking the cloth from his eyes, and looks out into the room. He sees Hoodrat sitting in a chair across from him, apparently watching him. He sees Sekhmet Baset intently looking at him, now seeing that she was actually a female. He sees another woman sitting in front of a pretty high tech d.i.y. computer station and server, wearing dark shades, and her locked hair wrapped up in a head wrap, the t-shirt that she's wearing emblazoned with the Eye of Heru. He then sees a male figure also sternly staring at him, and becomes quite shocked; The Black Fist was standing right in front of him! His eyes widen, not being able to hide his shock. "What the-...?!", was all he could get out.

"How are you feeling?", The Black Fist asks.
"...I've been better..."

"...Sorry for the rough treatment." The Black Fist then turns to Sekhmet Baset, shooting her a dirty look, "Things didn't go as planned..."

"...Apparently", he says, holding onto his ribs.

He turns back to the young Mystery Man. "We brought you here to help you heal up."

"...And, where exactly is *here*?"

"...The heart of the revolution."

"What?!?!", he tries to control his shock. *I'm at The Black Fist's base of operations?!?!*

"Be glad...", Hoodrat sarcastically says, "You got *any* idea *how long* it me, and my crew to be invited up in here...?!"

"...Hoodie...", The Black Fist starts.

"...-Shuttin' up", Hoodrat sheepishly returns.

"So, brother...", The Black Fist says, now becoming more direct, "...Who are you?"

He briefly pauses, getting his bearings back. "...Just another souljah trying to protect the streets."

"...Is that right?"

"You can't do it all alone...nor *should* you."

"Oh?", The Black Fist returns, raising an eyebrow behind his sports goggles.

"Look....", he says, becoming more serious and solemn, "...I ain't no saint. I've done my dirt. Five years ago...? I was doing a stint in juvie for doing my dirt. Then, I heard stories about one man out there, cleaning up the streets of all the knuckleheads, and dirty cops." He slightly pauses. "After that...I wanted to change."

"Really? Just like that...?"

"Look...the streets took everything else from me. My moms...my pops...", he slightly

pauses, "...My best friend."

The Black Fist slightly pauses, becoming a bit unnerved. He was telling a familiar story,

one that he's heard too often. It was also starting to hit a little bit too close to home,

bringing back unpleasant past memories, especially of Jabari. Wanting the young

warrior to continue on with his story, he asks a leading question, a tactic that he'd

learned from Nzinga. "How were they all taken from you..?", he asks.

"Some stickup kid killed my pops when I was nine...it was a robbery gone bad. Moms

couldn't handle it, and got caught up in the drug game. She O.D.'ed when I was

thirteen." He slightly pauses. "My boy was runnin' the streets with me. He got popped

by some dealer while I was locked up."

"...Sorry to hear that."

"...Don't be. I had my chances...I just ain't take 'em, at the time. Used to be down with

this community program...." He pauses, annoyed with himself, "...I ain't stick wit it."

His story was making The Black Fist feel more and more uncomfortable. The

Sankofa-Ifa Community Center had youth programs to keep the neighborhood children

off the streets, and tried to steer them into more constructive cultural, and community oriented endeavors. Not many of the children ended up following through with the programs; whether Rites of Passage, warrior training, or just community service. It disheartened him to hear that yet another young person had fallen to the wayside. It hurt him even worse, as he *really* started to remind him of Jabari, now. "What changed your mind...?", The Black Fist asks.

"...My boy Jamel gettin' blasted." He pauses, shaking his head. "That was the last straw, for me. This ain't the life."

"..I feel ya, bro", Hoodrat says.

"..Started to hear about what you was doin' on the streets...takin' on the dirty cops and the knuckleheads. Started to do some reading while I was still inside. Made me wanna change..."

"...Quite honorable...", Sekhmet Baset says, "...Perhaps I was wrong to engage you..."

"...Ya think?!"

"What's your name, brother..?", The Black Fist asks, trying to steer the conversation back.

"...Ain't got one. Like I said...I'm just another souljah trying to save the streets."

"Then...what's your government name?"

"...Cabral Davila", he finally says, after a long pause, "...Junior."

The Black Fist stiffens up, as he tries to hide his shock, the eeriness of this encounter.

He's Cab's son!!!, he breathes to himself. His family were loyal supporters of the organization from the community; immigrants from Cape Verde on his dad's side, and Brazil on his mother's, who were raised here. They were always highly supportive of their efforts, and continued that support even when the organization began to falter after the riots. They were also close to Jabari's own family, as well. It was disheartening to see the way that all of these families had fallen apart, due to crime and drugs. He actually remembered seeing Cab, Jr. at a few of the organization's events and programs; so young and innocent, so full of life. To see him so embittered at such a young age, it haunted Nyerere to no end. "Fist...", Amirah comments, full of concern, "...You okay?".

"...I'm...fine. It was just a little hard to hear."

"...A common story, here in New Washington City", Hoodrat dryly comments.

"...You ain't lying", Amirah sadly adds.

"Thems the breaks...", Cab, Jr. returns.

"So...", The Black Fist asks, "What got you locked up?"

"Gun charge...", Cab Jr. returns, after a long pause, "...Some street punks were messin' wit me and Jamel. Felt that we needed some protection." He pauses again, becoming sour. "Fuckin' cops profiled us...WWB...frisked us both...caught me with the gat. Sent me to juvie after that. I was fifteen..." He angrily pauses, again. "Jamel got blasted not long after that..."

Amirah takes a short intake of breath, remembering the case. Jamel Bowman was yet another body that she was trying to tie to Donnell "Black Caesar" Fennel, and his drug crew back then. She had heard about Black Caesar trying to forcibly recruit local kids from the neighborhood into his crew, and the dire consequences for the ones that didn't join. It hurt her deeply to hear Cab, Jr.'s story, especially about her inability to catch the people that were responsible for Jamel's death. The same thoughts were probably swimming around The Black Fist's head, causing his level of discomfort to increase. He shakes it off, and then becomes quite stern with him. "You could have gotten yourself killed out there...", he dresses down Cab, Jr.

"Yo...", Cab, Jr. says, now becoming defensive, "...I can't help it of this chucklehead and his crew messed me up...!"

"...-Hey!", Hoodrat says, now becoming insulted.

"...If you knew what you were doing...", The Black Fist fires back, "...They never would have been able *to* sneak up on you!"

"...That's right!", Hoodrat says, now feeling vindicated.

"...-Please!", Cab, Jr. derisively comments, "...They a buncha rookies...taggin' up walls after they're done, like a buncha kids! This ain't no game!"

"...-*They* know how to listen, and they work as a team!", The Black Fist fires back.

"...-They're *clowns*!"

"...-They're also not stupid enough to go out there without any type of protection!"

"...-I can handle myself!"

"...Yeah...", The Black Fist dryly responds, "...You've *really* proven that to us, tonight..."

"...-Fist!", Amirah exclaims, shocked.

"This ain't just about busting the heads of the predators from within! You also have the unseen hand guiding the chaos from the *outside*!"

"Man...*what*?!", Cab, Jr. asks, exasperated.

The Black Fist just pauses, disappointedly shaking his head. Cab, Jr. was just too raw with rage, too undisciplined to understand the depths of the struggle. He wasn't ready to be out there on the streets, too unprepared to face the dangers that were out there. "...You're not ready to do this", he flatly states.

"Man, what?!?!", Cab, Jr. says, shocked, "What are you talking about?!?!"

"...You have *no* idea what you're getting yourself into!"

"Wha'chu mean?!?!"

"...-This is *bigger* than just the street dealers, and dirty cops! *Much* bigger!" The Black Fist angrily pauses. "You're *not* ready for this!"

"What?!?!", Cab, Jr. angrily responds, "...And this clown, and his crew *is*?!?!"

"...-*They've* already proven to me that they're ready, and down for the cause! *You* haven't!"

Cab, Jr. pauses, becoming angered. He'd wanted the respect and blessings of The Black Fist, to welcome him into the struggle, and embrace him as a brother and comrade. Unfortunately, he was being shut down by him...and pretty hard, too. At the same time, he was reflecting on his last few missions, and how poorly he'd done on his own. Perhaps he *wasn't* ready to do this...at least, not on *his own*. He momentarily pauses, reflecting on his options. He *definitely* wasn't trying to run with Hoodrat, and his crew; that would be a slap in his face. *But*...he needed to get better, and learn how to be in the struggle, the *right* way. Perhaps... "Then...why don't you teach me?", he solemnly asks The Black Fist.

"*What*...?!?!", The Black Fist asks, totally shocked, caught off guard by his question.

"...Teach me!", Cab, Jr. says, "...I wanna learn how to do this right. I gotta learn *somehow*..."

"Oh, wooooord...?!", Hoodrat asks.

"...Will you teach me?", Cab, Jr. reiterates, "...Make me a better souljahr out there on the streets...?"

"This ain't a club...", The Black Fist starts, "...We're not looking for membership-..."

"...-Fist", Amirah interjects, "...Sidebar, please..."

The Black Fist pauses, swallowing what he was going to say. He then lets out a heavy sigh, and exits with Amirah. They walk over to a section of the warehouse that he uses as a separate training room. They walk far away enough to be out of earshot, and then turn to each other. The Black Fist pulls down his sports goggles, and Amriah looks him deep into his eyes, a very concerned look on her face. "Fist, what's wrong...?", she asks.

"...He's *not* ready to be out there."

"...Is *he* not ready...or, are *you* not ready?"

"*What*?!?!", he asks, shocked.

"This isn't about him...this is about Jabari."

The Black Fist pauses, trying to hold a stoic expression. "Jabari's got *nothing* to do with this-..."

"...-He's got *everything* to do with this!"

The Black Fist looks away, his face betraying his feelings. "I'm *not* looking for a mwanafundzi-..."

"...-This is different. He's *not* Jabari. Cab will listen to you...Jabari *didn't*."

"...-Jabari *died* because of me!"

"...-Jabari died because Black Caesar was a maniac! He'd also made his own bed. There was *nothing* that you could've done about that..."

The Black Fist pauses for a long time, letting it all sink in. "Okay...."

"He wants to learn....and wants to learn from *you*. That's the most important thing to him."

The Black Fist pauses, and lets all that has been said sink in. He could always use another revolutionary associate in his battles with the powers that be, especially if he had to go abroad; there could always be someone around that he can trust to watch over the homefront, while he was gone. Plus, he wasn't going to be around forever, and needed to have someone to pass the torch to, and carry on the struggle. Hoodrat was cool, and he liked his crew, but they weren't really his type of generals, and torch carriers. With *Cab, Jr.*, on the other hand...there were some possibilities. He was already familiar with some of Africana P.R.I.D.E.'s teachings and philosophy, as well as having been exposed to some of their programs. Perhaps this *could* work, with the proper guidance...? "You really think so...?", he finally asks Amirah.

"...Couldn't think of anyone better to teach him."

"...Without the next generation to carry on the struggle, the struggle will die."

"Exactly."

"I see your point."

"...*You* were the one to teach me that. Just needed to remind you of that, from time to time.

"I hear ya", he finally says, now smiling.

They both share a smile, their affection for each other growing. It was great for them to be able to bond like this, and to be able to support each other about decisions, such as this. The Black Fist gently strokes her face, and they share a smile. They give each other a quick peck on the lips, and head back out of the room, joining the others in the control room, The Black Fist replacing his sports goggles back onto his face.

The others all look over to them, now filled with anticipation. Cab, Jr. looks over at them, trying to hold a determined look on his face, but was having a hard time trying to maintain that look. He desperately hoped that the Black Fist would take him up on his offer, and take him on as his mwanafundzi. To be a student under him would be of the highest honor, and would be his way to contribute to the struggle. "One last time...", The Black Fist addresses Cab, Jr., "...*Why* do you want to do this...?".

"...I wanna do my part to help protect my community, and my peoples. We've suffered enough."
"Will you dedicate yourself to defend our people from the predators...both from outside the community, and from within?"
"...Yes!"
"Okay...", The Black Fist finally says, after a long pause, "...Welcome to the struggle...brother."

Cab, Jr. break out into a smile, no longer being able to hide his emotions. If his ribs didn't hurt so much, he would be jumping up and down, jubilantly celebrating. "We've got *a lot* of work ahead of us...", The Black Fist starts.

"...I'm ready!"

"...You *better* be! I'm not going to take it easy on you."

"I'm down for this...*trust* me."

"Firstly...welcome to the Freedman's Underground Revolutionary Initiative...or FURI for

short..."

"...I'm honored to be here."

"See...you says that *now*...", Hoodrat starts. The others snicker behind him, causing Cab

to raise his eyebrow at them.

"What's so funny...?"

"See....you haven't actually *trained* with him, yet..."

"Oh...?" Cab gets a sinking feeling in his stomach. *Am I going to regret this...?*

"Lets just say...me and my crew are straight. *You* can do all that crap he wants you to

do."

"...Wimp", The Black Fist jokes with him.

"Nah...", Hoodrat laughs, "...*You* be trying to kill a brotha!"

"Okay, first things first...", Amirah interjects, "We're gonna need a way to get in contact

with you..."

"Okay..."

"Here...", she says, passing him one of the phones, "...I just programmed it for you. It's how we communicate with each other."

"...Cool...", Cab says, inspecting the phone.

"...We'll be handling your training here", The Black Fist says, "You can keep your own spot for yourself....as well as an additional safehouse for FURI purposes..."

"...I'm down wit that!"

"Training won't be easy, *but*...I'm willing to teach you everything you want to know."

"I want this...*trust* me. I'm down."

The Black Fist broadly smiles. Perhaps this wasn't going to be such a bad thing, after all? In training Cab, maybe he could finally find some personal redemption in what he couldn't accomplish with Jabari? Cab was dedicated to the struggle, and was more than willing to learn. Besides, it would be nice to go out into the field with a partner every once in a while, if not on a consistent basis.

He extends his hand out to Cab, and smiles at him. "Welcome to the revolution...". Cab smiles back, and takes his hand, shaking it in return.

CHAPTER 27

Nzinga was sitting at her desk, not in the best of moods. The election results had been coming in all day, and the numbers weren't looking good...at least, not to her. A. Simi Leishon-Integration was on his way to yet another landslide victory, thoroughly trouncing his opponent for his mayoral seat. It looked like it was going to be yet *another* four years of hard times for the locals, while all of the transplants, hipsters, and big businesses were going to continue to flourish, and thrive in the city that formerly belonged to the people. It thoroughly displeased her, and made her feel a bit disillusioned. More and more, she thought about moving on to something else, to taking on other opportunities to further her career. Perhaps it *was* time to leave? At the same time, she deeply loved the city, and how she was able to grow here. She'd made some dear friends here, especially her friendship with Nyerere, and loved the feeling of camaraderie that she'd developed with the activist community, as well as the city's residents. She had given them a voice that they sorely needed, and a platform to air their grievances. Could she *really* turn her back on all of that...?

Malachi makes his way over to her desk, an uncomfortable look pasted on his golden face. This causes her eyebrows to furrow, not seeing him acting like his normal, jovial self. This caused the pit of her stomach to knot up. "Uh ohhh...", she begins, not liking the sinking feeling that she was getting.

"I take it that you've seen the election results, right...?"

"Yeah...", she sourly returns, "...Unfortunately...."

"Well...guess what?"

""No...", she winces, shaking her head, "...Oh, dear *god*, no...!"

"Yep....Jackson wants us to go cover his victory party at his campaign headquarters."

"Aw, man...!", she angrily fumes.

"Unfortunately...it's news."

"...Damn! Can't he send someone else...?!"

"...-Not a request!" He briefly pauses. "Jackson's own words...not mine."

Nzinga rolls her eyes, now pouting. Her editor Jackson *knows* how much she despises the man, and felt that it was cruel and unusual punishment for him to send her to cover his election win. She lets out a heavy sigh, and starts to gather her personal effects. "Alright, alright...", she wearily says, "...I'm coming". Malachi heavily sighs as well, empathizing with her. Neither of them liked the man, and despised his politics. He had sold out the community to curry favor from the Powers That Be, and had no second thoughts about it. The so-called change that he'd promised to bring to the city, never came for those who desperately needed that change. They both slowly gathered their things, and finally make their way out of the door. As they head towards the elevator,

Nzinga was really starting to reconsider an offer extended to her by a friend who was working at a new Digital Television Channel that had recently aired. They were looking for people to fill their news media department, and he had dropped her name to the executives there. Perhaps it *was* time to move on...? As the elevators doors were closing, maybe so was her time here in New Washington City...

*   *   *   *   *

Cab was feeling all types of sore, soaking his body in some herbal ointment that Nefertara had recommended to him. Both she and Nyerere had been pushing him quite hard, putting him through some intense training. He was soaking his body in this bath, hoping to alleviate some of the pain that he was feeling in his body. He was also taking the time to let his mind relax. It shocked him to find out who The Black Fist really was; he had no clue that it could have been Nyerere. Even more shocking, was finding out who Sekhmet Baset was, and that she was actually a healer. The more he learned, the more enthralled he became. He was grateful to have been accepted into the fold, and become a part of the movement. The more that he learned about how FURI functioned, the more determined he became to excel in his training. He not only wanted to make the others proud of him, he was even more determined to protect the city and its residents from all those that would do harm to her. He thoroughly hated those powers that be, and how they'd subjugated the city for generations...all for there own personal enrichment.

Nyerere was right about the unseen hand guiding the darkness that plagued the city, and elsewhere. They needed to be stopped...at any, and all costs. He was looking forward to eventually taking them all down; PTB, Unlimited...The System...O. Pression Enterprises, Unlimited...Iggy Norance and his family's empire...Ray Sysm and *his* family's empire...Wyatt Supremacy, and his political allies....*all* were going to be made to pay.

Cab smiled to himself, despite the pain. It was a *good* sore feeling, as far as he was concerned. He was learning so much about the different African fighting styles; both continental, and diasporic, as well as gaining training in survivalist skills. Not only were they expanding his consciousness culturally and physically, but also politically and spiritually as well. They'd helped him to build his own ancestral alter in his own hideout, to worship and communicate with his parents, as well as any other ancestors that he wanted to reach out to. They also had him doing reading assignments, though he'd resisted a bit, at first. He needed to learn and know more about our people's history, and struggles, if he were to get more involved in it; learn from the successes and mistakes made from revolutionary elders and ancestors of the past, in order to move forward. The fun part, though, was the hands on training. He battled a bit with Nyerere over the music that he trained to, leaning more towards some harder edged Hip Hop tracks, as opposed to the drumming music that Nyerere would rather have him listen to. They compromised a bit, choosing to play a lot of revolutionary and conscious rap music, to help enhance his training sessions.

It amazed him how many fighting styles still existed from his warrior ancestors; Dambe, Laamb, Nuba wrestling, Shackle Hands, La Lutte, Musangwe, Hikuta, Kipura, Ngolo, Zulu Impi, Kamangula, Ladja, Gidigbo...and those were just some of the *hand-to-hand* fighting styles! Weapons training was just as intense, as Nyerere put him through the paces teaching him stickfighting and sword fighting, and other types of weapons training. Amirah scared him to death with her deadly sharpshooting skills, and vowed never to piss her off, or get on her bad side. It took him a minute to warm up to her, considering her role as a police officer; the fact that she's the brains and glue behind this whole operation really impressed him. She had thoroughly earned his respect for her, and he looked to her as a second guide, and sister figure. His spirit was growing lighter, and his rage was now more focused, being able to channel all of that energy into his warrior training. He looked forward to being able to eventually hit the streets, and take down some agents of The System.

It really irritated Cab how the so-called Black political machine of the city was really in it only for themselves, and *not* the upliftment of the community. While they gained prestige and grew prosperous, the rest of the city was going downhill, or being sold out to special interests from outside of the community. His own hatred for A. Simi, and his ilk started to grow immensely, vowing to take them all down, as well. *Dirty buncha sellouts...*, he fumes to himself,*...Ain't no better than those that already been oppressing us all along....* It just made him all that more determined to complete his training, and fight them until his last breath. As the weeks have passed, he'd became ever more vigilant in his growth as a warrior, and now truly understood what this war was about. He'd even grown to have more respect for Hoodrat and CJZC; their contributions to the struggle was just as important as his, and they'd proven to be worthy allies and comrades. They aided in his training, and helped to keep him grounded. They were all souljahrs in the struggle, and were all needed to help protect the streets of New Washington City from all of the predators...both from outside, and from within.

CHAPTER 28

Dusk had already come, and the night sky covered the city, as Iggy Norace was sitting in his office. He was happy to hear about A. Simi's election win, as he knew that it would happen, as they'd planned it. The residents were so ridiculously childish and gullible, that they truly looked at A. Simi as some sort of savior, or messiah come to lead them to some promised land. He smiles to himself, shaking his head, almost laughing out loud. He takes a long drag from his cigar, holds it in, and then takes as long exhale, the smoke billowing from his aged lips. For the most part, life was very good. All was going according to plan, and none of the city's residents were the wiser. The murders of their associates had stopped, so they were satisfied for that reprieve. At the same time, they'd never caught whoever it was that was taking out their people and associates, nor did they ever find out who it was. It didn't make him feel uneasy; just highly annoyed. The fact that this person was able to get away with this made him question the effectiveness of his operatives.

He takes another long drag from his cigar, his mind now wandering. The gentrification of the city was going at a slower pace than he'd expected. He'd always had an issue with patience, and that personality flaw was surfacing at the moment. Even with the flooding of the streets with these guns, it wasn't clearing out the riff raff fast enough for him. This city was going to be theirs again, and it was going to happen *now*.

Perhaps he need a wider reach...? Or, better yet...maybe he might need some outside

help with this...? His mind starts to wander again, and then an evil smile spreads across

his face. *Yes, of course...*, he thinks to himself, *why didn't I think of contacting him*

before...?. They were great business partners, and their families had always worked well

together in the past. Besides...*he* has a reach that surpasses even *his own*. Yes...this

would *definitely* be a business deal that he'd be interested in. He continues to wear that

evil smile, and starts to nod to himself. Time to bring in some reinforcements...

He presses his buzzer, summoning his secretary. After a few seconds, she replies

to him. "Yes, Mr. Norance...?", she asks.

"...Contact my pilot, and tell him to have the jet ready to take off."

"Yes, sir. When would you like to leave?"

"...Within the hour."

"...And, where will you be going, sir?"

"...Europe. I have an old friend that I need to discuss some business with..."

"...Yes, sir. Right away, sir."

*   *   *   *   *

Cab tried his best to contain the smile that he wanted to so proudly plant on his face. After several months of training, he was finally being initiated into the fold. Dressed in all white, he was finally going to be initiated as a warrior, and truly be a part of F.U.R.I., and the movement. The scents of Sage, and Frankincense & Myrrh filled the air, the room surrounded by candles, and the various deities of war. His body was oiled down, and chants were made, and he could feel the energies converging inside of him. He'd felt a renewed sense of purpose, and a sense of burning calm at the same time. He was glad that Nefertara and Hoodrat had come out for the ceremony, and had shown him support. He had earned their respect as well, and were glad to see him achieve this rite of passage. Nyerere had organized a beautiful ceremony, and Cab felt very moved by it. Amirah just smiled, proud to see Cab achieve this rite, considering all of the misery that he'd gone through in his younger days. To see him be able to come so far was a blessing, in and of itself.

He had chosen his own weapons as a warrior; a pair of Rungu throwing clubs. He had watched a video once of how the Zulu and Masai used their battle mace and clubs in combat, and felt that they would be an excellent weapon to have out on the streets. Though his marksmanship had improved tremendously under Amirah's excellent supervision, like Nyerere, Cab had also chosen not to carry a gun out on the streets. Carrying the Black Star *throwing stars*, however, he could definitely swing with that. He was shaping up to be a fine warrior, and Nyerere was glad to have taken him on as his mwanafundzi. He'd felt a sense of redemption, having taken on Cab as a mwanafundzi, guiding him on his journey to become a warrior. He'd just wished that Jabari could have been able to take the *same* path, instead of having been lured towards the streets, and meeting such a violent end. At least, he was able to save *one* young soul, and get them to commit to the struggle. The movement was growing, and he didn't feel as alone as he did, when he'd first started on this journey. Now, there were others to join with him in the struggle against the Powers That Be, and protect their people and community from all the ills that try to oppress, and suppress them. Both men's hearts were becoming lighter, and more optimistic. Cab was an excellent mwanafundzi, and a dedicated warrior. With his training and initiation over with, it was now time to take action, and take their battle to the streets.

Cab was putting on his own uniform, his familiar baggy green pants, and short sleeved red hoodie. The Black Fist approaches him, fully dressed, carrying a package. Cab looks up at him, somewhat surprised, and stands up straight. "What's up...?", he asks.

"...Wanted to give you something...for completing your initiation."
"...Really?!"
"...Yep." He hands him the package, a slight smirk on his face. "Here..."

Cab takes the package, bewildered, and opens it. His eyes widen, and he looks up at The Black Fist, his face full of shock. "For real...?!", he asks.

"...Yep. You earned it."

"Seriously?!"

"...Welcome to the movement...ndugu."

Cab couldn't believe his eyes. The Black Fist had given him his own sweater vest with the 'power fist' symbol on it, as well as a pair of wristbands with the revolutionary colors on them, and the continent of Africa. He was so moved, that he didn't even know what to say. He takes a deep breath, and puts the sweater vest on, as well as the wristbands. He felt even more energized, as he put the items on, feeling their power and energy. He sports a confident smile on his face, and gathers the rest of his uniform. The Black Fist smiles in return, giving him the once over. "...Not bad", he says. Cab turns towards a reflective surface, and models the new gear. He looked much better than he ever did in his original uniform, the black power fist symbol now prominently displayed on his chest. Added to the fact that the months of training helped him to build up his muscle mass, he truly looked like a warrior. His chest swelled with pride, now ready to take on the world, and all of her miscreants at one time.

Cab dons his red baseball cap and black eye mask, ready to take to the streets.

Amirah begins to set up the computer station, ready to assist them as they head out. She pauses briefly, and turns to Cab. "So...", she asks, "...Have you chosen a name for yourself?".

"Honestly...? I hadn't thought about it."

"Neither did I, when I first started...", The Black Fist confesses.

"You deserve a warrior name", Amirah says.

"...I'm just another souljah trying to protect the streets."

"Hmmm...", The Black Fist says, after a moment, "...It fits."

"What does?"

"...D'Street Souljahr."

Cab pauses. "You think so...?"

"...It suits you."

Cab pauses, smiling to himself. "I like it."

"Great!", Amirah says, smiling, "Baddies beware...D'Street Souljahr is here!"

"...Now I *really* like it!"

"Okay gentlemen...", Amirah says, turning back to the computer console, and putting on her headset, "...Let's get this show on the road! Comms in."

Both men put their bluetooth earpieces in their ears. They look at each other, and share a smile, nodding to each other. "You ready to do this...?", The Black Fist asks.

"...You know it!", D'Street Souljahr replies.

"...Let's go!"

They give each other a fist bump, and out the skylight they go, disappearing into the night. Amirah smiles to herself as they leave, tracking their signals, and pulling up schematics of the city's streets. *Look out world...*, she proudly thinks,...*here comes the revolution!*.

EPILOGUE

Ife Ochoa was beaming, happy to be holding her shrine house's Orisha Festival at the Sankofa-Ifa Community Center. The house where her shrine house usually operated out of had their water main explode, and flooded out their basement and first floor, causing them to seek an alternative location to hold services, and their event. The Uhuru Shule Academy already had an event scheduled for that same night, so it was unavailable; Nyerere had talked to Mama Tablua and Baba Balogun as a favor to her, and they'd graciously welcomed them, and offered the services of the center to her shrine house. Ife was eternally grateful to all that Africana P.R.I.D.E. provided for her, and always supporting her in her time of need. The center was beautifully decorated, adorned with the images and idols of the different orishas, splashed with the colors representing the various divinity that they prayed to. The festival was well under way, with drumming, singing, and sacred dances being performed for the different orishas that they worshiped; representing for the practitioners of the various faiths of Santería, Lukúmí, Candomblé, and Yoruba. Food had been made available to all that wanted to come and celebrate with them, and experience this event. Ife herself was beaming with joy, dressed in the colors of her orisha, Yemeya. She scans the crowd, and sees the joyous faces of the revelers and their guests, all of them enjoying the festivities. Her eyes catch Mama Tabula, dressed in the colors of her own orisha of Oshun, smiles at her, and makes her way over to her. They graciously greet each other, hugging and kissing each other on the cheek. "Modupe, Mama Tablua", Ife coos, "Thank you *so* much for all of your help". Mama Tabula just brightly beams in return.

"You're very welcome, dear sister. Anything that we could do to help."

"We were afraid that we might have to cancel the festival."

"...All the more reason that we're so glad to be able to help you hold it here."

"I'm glad that the members of your shrine house were able to make it."

"...We wouldn't have missed this for the world, dear sister!"

They joyfully hug again, and turn their attentions back to the party. All in attendance were enjoying themselves, feeling safe, and having a good time. The rhythm of the drums pulsated throughout the building, reverberating through all in attendance, taking it out on the dance floor. Ife momentarily pauses, and then turns back to Mama Tabula. "Have you seen Nyerere, Mama Tabula...?", she asks, "He promised that he was going to stop in...?".

"...Actually, he just called. He says that he's running late though..."

"Oh...?", Ife asks, growing concerned, "...What happened? Is everything alright...?"

"...Oh, it's nothing serious, sister. Just wrapping up some business with some academic colleagues..."

"Oh, okay", Ife responds, relieved, "That's good. As long as he's doing alright..."

"No problem, sister", Tabula guffaws, "It's all good. He's been doing quite well...you don't have to worry about that."

Ife was glad to hear that Nyerere had been in better spirits as of late. She remembered the hell that he'd caught as director of the Uhuru Shule Academy, and was glad that his spirits had improved when he moved on, and pursued his academic career. Though she missed him terribly as a co-worker, she was glad to see him achieving his career goals, and succeeding in life, and being *happy*. *I hope that his business won't keep him away for too long*, Ife thinks to herself, *I wonder who he's meeting with...?* She masks her worried thoughts, sending up a silent prayer for his protection, and then joins the others in the celebrating.

*   *   *   *   *

The Black Fist has made his way to the docks, located southeast of the Warehouse District, having ridden in the *Queen Amina*. The info that he and Amirah had gotten through FURI's contacts was that those weapons were a prototype hybrid of different weapons makers from around the world, and were penetrating into the black market, and that a shipment of those weapons was supposed to be shipping out of the docks tonight. He parks the *Queen Amina*, and uses Parkour to make his approach, undetected. "I'm on the scene...", he gravelly responds, "Making my way over to the loading winches".

"...Roger that", Amirah responds, ready at her station.

He makes his way over to some nearby trailers, and as he shows up, he hears a ruckus going on, on the docks themselves, with the familiar sounds of flesh being pounded, and screams of pain. He makes his way over the top of some trailers, and gets a better view of the scene from higher ground. He is shocked by what he sees. "What the-...?", is all that he's able to get out. Amirah hears the shock in his voice, and calls out to him through his earpiece, full of concern.

"Fist...", she asks, "What's going on...?"

"...Somebody beat me here..."

"What?! *Who*?!"

The Black Fist watches on, as he sees two black females engaged in combat with the dock workers and port security, introducing them into a world of hurt. He sees their dark caramel forms spin kick, punch, and slash about acrobatically, battering their combatants with impunity using Juego de Maní; with one using a machete, and the other using a wooden staff. Both women are dressed in white pants, and beaded jewelry of the orishas; with one wearing the official Puerto Rican flag as a headwrap and halter top, while the other wears the Nationalist Puerto Rican flag as a headwrap and sleeveless tank top. The Black Fist watches them in shock, witnessing the carnage that they're inflicting on the dock workers and port security guards. "...It's Bomba and Plena", he finally answers.

"...The twins?! *Here*?!"
"...Apparently."

He momentarily watches their prowess in combat, highly impressed, with both of the women being highly trained maniseros, and then decides to join the battle, not wanting to leave his revolutionary sisters alone in combat. He detaches the clubs from the back of his belt, and leaps into action, joining into the fray. "I'm going in", he calls out.

"...I'll call for backup, just in case!"
"...-Just be on standby! This might be over quick."

He batters the other combatants about, switching fighting styles, adding to their pain and misery, cutting them down with his darts and throwing stars, coming in from their blind side. Bomba and Plena momentarily turn in his direction, surprised to see him, and then continue to batter their opponents about. The three warriors bring mayhem and misery to all that chose to cross their paths, opening up a world of hurt and pain on them. The

Black Fist flings about his darts and throwing stars, disarming the port security officers, and dock workers alike. Battered bodies are strewn all over the docks, enveloping this chaotic scene, illuminated by the bright lights of the port.

The three combatants victoriously stand over their opponents, all of them battered and strewn about the docks. They look around, scanning the scene, making sure that none were left to mount a sneak attack, once their guard was dropped, or warn any others as to their presence. They briefly pauses, and then turn to greet each other. "Hola, comadres...", The Black Fist replies, a slight smirk on his face, "...Bienvenido a mi cuidad".

"Encantada, hermano...", Bomba greets, sheathing her machete, "Gracias por su ayuda."

"...De nada, hermana."

"Comó estás, hermano...?", Plena asks, smiling, "...Estás bien?"

"Sí, sí...mucho mejor, ahora..."

"Fist...", Amirah calls into his earpiece, "...Is everything alright...?"

"...Fine, Amirah", he says, "We just wrapped up our little party. Stand down from akoben status."

"...Roger that!"

"Quien es...?", they ask in unison.

"...Mi hermana revolucionista. She's my partner here, and helps me."

"Ah...okay", Bomba says.

"We should get out of here...", he says after a moment, "...Get away from prying eyes...compare notes..."

"...Adonde?", they ask in unison, a bewildered look shared on their faces.

"...I know a place. Follow me..."

They make their way across the shadows, and sneak off into the night. The Black Fist was glad to actually have some help in cleaning up the streets, and now with his overseas contacts here in the city, he *knew* that something big was going down. He'd been feeling a dark presence as of late, but couldn't put his finger on what, or who. The *last* thing that he needed was some new players in the game; it was either that, or Iggy Norance and his bunch were up to no good with some new diabolical plan. Either way, he needed to be ready to take on whatever was to come.

TO BE CONTINUED....

THE END

ABOUT THE AUTHOR

KEVIN ALBERTO SABIO is an author and activist, born and raised in Brooklyn, New York. He is the youngest child of Honduran Garifuna immigrant parents. He attended Newbury College studying Mass Communications, and graduated from Southern Connecticut State University with a B.S. in Video Productions. He is the founder and organizer of the **Universal Africana Literary Arts Movement**.

Mr. Sabio is the author of: *"Raise Your Brown Black Fist: The Political Shouts of an Angry Afro Latino"* (Authorhouse, 2010), *"Raise Your Brown Black Fist 2: MORE Political Shouts of an Angry Afro Latino"* (Outskirts Press, 2011), *"In My Lifetime: Funny Stories of Life Experiences"* (Outskirts Press, 2014), *"The Chronicles of The Black Fist"* (CreateSpace, 2015), *"Demure Nights"* (CreateSpace, 2015), *"Spittin' Lyrics N Waxin' Poetic"* (Draft2Digital, 2015), *"Drum Speaking: Tales From an Inner City Griot"* (CreateSpace, 2016), *"Seductra, Web of Desire"*, (CreateSpace, 2017), and *"Fiesta Girl"* (Draft2Digital, 2018). This is his tenth book.

Mr. Sabio has profiles on social media websites such as LinkedIn, G+, Facebook, and Twitter. You can also follow his literary activities through his blog *"The Chronicles of the Brown Black Fist"* at www.brownblackfistchronicles.blogspot.com. You can also join his author Fan Page on Facebook at www.facebook.com/AuthorKevinSabio. Booking requests, and audience feedback can be sent via email to Brownblackfist.book@gmail.com. Mr. Sabio currently resides in Wilmington, DE.

53911513R00118